'You gave me your word eleven months ago.'

'And you gave me yours. I am not the one planning to break my vows.'

For an age they simply stared at each other, neither bending. The tension between them had become so thick a steak knife would have had trouble cutting through it. Yet Nicolai could not help but admire her. There were not many people brave enough to face him off.

Rosa caved in first. Extending her hand, she said, 'We will shake on it. One month, Nicolai. And if at the end you refuse to give me my divorce then I will show you just how dirty *I* can play.'

Her fiery declaration sent a frisson of excitement racing through his veins. As he reached for her hand he realised it was the first time their flesh had touched since they had exchanged their rings.

And as he walked back down the stairs, victory still ringing within him, Nico realised it had also been the first time he had set foot in her suite since she had moved in.

Michelle Smart's love affair with books began as a baby, when she would cuddle them in her cot. This love for all things wordy has never left her. A voracious reader of all genres, her love of romance was cemented at the age of twelve when she came across her first Mills & Boon® book. That book sparked a seed and, although she didn't have the words to explain it then, she discovered something special—that a book had the capacity to make her heart beat as if she were falling in love.

When not reading, or pretending to do the housework, Michelle loves nothing more than creating worlds of her own featuring handsome brooding heroes and the sparkly, feisty women who can melt their frozen hearts. She hopes her books can make her readers' hearts beat a little faster too.

Michelle Smart lives in Northamptonshire with her own hero and their two young sons.

This is Michelle's stunning debut—
we hope you love it as much as we do!

Visit www.millsandboon.co.uk

THE RINGS
THAT BIND

BY
MICHELLE SMART

MILLS & BOON

THE RINGS
THAT BIND

To Gilly

CHAPTER ONE

Rosa Baranski sat on the kitchen worktop, ostensibly waiting for the coffee percolator to finish, and gazed down at the slate tiles. She hated the flooring. Even with the benefit of under-floor heating it always felt so cold.

It was incredible to think she had once lived in a house of the same proportions as the place she currently called home. In that, her first children's home, she had shared the house with forty other children and an ever-rotating shift of adults. The home had been a hub of noise and chaos, something she had hated until she had discovered how terrifying silence could be and how loneliness could destroy your soul.

Back then, her bedroom had been around the same size as the one she had now. Then, she had shared it with four other girls.

In those dark days and nights she had dreamed of escape.

Around two decades on, and for entirely different reasons, she had come to the painful conclusion that she needed to escape again. At least now she had the power simply to leave.

But she could not do anything until she had spoken to Nico. However much her stomach churned at the thought, she could not leave without an explanation. It wouldn't be fair.

For what seemed the hundredth time she read the text message on her phone, her stomach twisting at the bland, almost curt words that leapt off the screen. It was from her brother.

She'd received it a week ago and could not stop reading it. She should delete it but she couldn't. It was her only tangible link to him.

Shifting her position in order to peer out of the window, she felt her belly do a funny skipping thing as she spotted the sleek black Maserati crunch slowly over the long gravel driveway before disappearing from view.

Nicolai was home.

The dread coursing through her bloodstream was reminiscent of the first time she had met him. She had attended an interview for the role of his temporary PA, providing maternity cover for his regular PA, who had gone into early labour.

She had sat in a large waiting room with five other potential candidates. She hadn't been able to help but notice that the secretary who had been placed in charge of them visibly braced herself every time she knocked on his office door. The other candidates must have noticed it too. All of them had sat in hushed, almost reverential silence.

If Nico Baranski's reputation had not already preceded him, the sight of the candidates' faces after they had been interviewed would have been enough to terrify them. One by one they left his office ashen-faced. One woman had been blinking back tears.

Rosa had been the last to go in.

By that point her nerves had been shredded.

She had entered the plush, masculine office and been confronted with an immovable body behind a huge oak desk and a hard, unwavering stare.

She had breathed a visible sigh of relief.

Far from the living embodiment of an ogre her febrile mind had conjured during the long wait for her turn, Nicolai Baranski was but a mere mortal. An enormously well-built, gorgeous mortal, but a mortal all the same.

Her relief had been so great her nerves had disappeared.

When he had finally spoken, inviting her to sit in rapid Russian, she had responded in kind without missing a single beat.

Only by the flicker of an eyebrow had he shown any response to her fluency.

'It says on your résumé that you studied Russian at university and then spent a year working in St Petersburg for the Danask Group after your graduation, before transferring back to London,' he had said, flipping through a pile of paper in front of him.

'That is correct.'

He looked up, the brilliance of his light green eyes piercing her. 'Your references are excellent. You are clearly a valued member of the Danask Group. Why do you want to leave?'

'I have gone as far as I can and I am looking for a new challenge. I have already worked my notice with them,' she added, knowing this position needed to be filled quickly.

'How many other jobs have you applied for?'

'None. This is the only one I thought suitable.'

'You do realise the job involves a lot of travel?'

'That is one of the reasons I applied.' The idea of escaping London and her deteriorating home life sounded wonderful. Not that she would say such a thing to him. Rosa kept a strict demarcation between her business and her personal life.

'You will often be required to leave the UK at short notice.'

'I will carry a travel case at all times for such eventualities.'

'You should know I am not interested in hiring someone who clock-watches.'

'I am aware of your reputation, Gaspadin Baranski,' she replied, matching his coolness of tone. 'You pay an excellent salary for good reason.'

He studied her with narrowed eyes before pulling a document wallet out of his top drawer and handing it to her. 'Translate that for me.'

The document was in Russian. She scanned it for a moment before translating. When she was done, Nico leaned back on his chair, a thoughtful expression on his face. 'When can you start?'

And that was it. The job had been hers. She had started immediately.

Now, she inhaled deeply and slowly, pulling the ponytail at the back of her head as tight as she could.

If there was one thing she had learned it was that when there was a potentially unpleasant job to do it was better to face it head-on. Get it over with. Even if it meant telling her husband news for which she had no way of knowing how he would react.

It wasn't until she heard movement from the door connecting the house with the underground garage that she snapped out of her stupor and jumped down, wincing as her bare feet hit the cold floor.

Shoving the phone into her pocket, she used all her powers of concentration to keep her hands steady and pour coffee into the waiting mug without spilling it everywhere.

Would he even bother seeking her out? Or would he hide away in his study as he so often did nowadays?

She listened to the sound of the study door being opened, followed less than a minute later by the sound of the same door closing. Muted footsteps grew closer until he was there, leaning nonchalantly against the kitchen doorframe, filling the space, arms folded across his broad chest.

'Hello, Rosa.'

'Hello, Nico.' She threw him a brief smile, praying he couldn't see the way her knees knocked together. Even though it was Sunday, and he had spent a good portion of the day travelling, he was impeccably dressed in a crisp white shirt, an incredibly snazzy silver-and-pink tie, and tailored dark grey trousers. It made her pale blue jogging bottoms and white T-shirt look positively grungy by comparison. 'Good trip?'

He considered, folding his arms across his chest. 'It could have been worse. I'm not yet convinced they are the kind of people I wish to do business with.'

Which undoubtedly meant he would *not* be investing in the mineral extraction facility he had spent the best part of a week scrutinising.

'Coffee?'

He nodded. 'Where's Gloria?' he asked, referring to their housekeeper.

She opened a cupboard and pulled a mug out. 'Her grandson has a bad dose of chicken-pox and she wants to give her daughter a break, so I've given her the weekend off.'

A furrow appeared on his brow. 'Why would you do that?'

Rosa rolled her eyes and poured coffee into the mug before adding a splash of milk. A few drops spilled onto the granite worktop. She wiped it absently with her wrist. 'I did it because she was worried about her daughter.'

'Her daughter is a fully grown woman.'

'That doesn't mean Gloria has abdicated her maternal feelings.' Not that Rosa knew anything about being the recipient of maternal feelings. Not since the age of five, when her mother had abandoned her. She held the mug out to him. 'Besides, it worked in my favour. I need to talk to you.' And she would prefer not to talk in front of an audience.

'That can wait for a minute. I have something for you.' Unfolding his arms, Nico produced a small gift-wrapped package and handed it to her, taking his mug in exchange. 'Happy birthday.'

Stunned at the gift—two days too late—she stared up at him. 'Thank you.'

His light green eyes sparkled. 'You're welcome. I'm sorry I didn't make it back in time to take you out.'

'Don't worry about it. Business comes first.' She tried to speak without rancour. Business always came first. In effect, their whole marriage was nothing more than a business transaction.

When she had agreed to what could only be described as a marriage of convenience, she could not have known there would come a point when something she accepted as part of the pact they had made would start to eat at her. She could not have known that something inside her would shift.

The idea of marriage—indeed, the deed itself—had come about in California. They had spent over a week there, working on the purchase of a mining facility. Once the final contract had been signed Nico had insisted on treating the whole team to a meal to celebrate.

They had been the last two standing. After ten days of continuous slog, Rosa had been ready to let her hair down. To her surprise, Nico had been in the mood to cut loose too.

When he'd suggested a drink in the bar that jutted out over the calm ocean she had readily agreed.

It was the first time they had been alone together in what could have been described as a social setting.

They had settled in a corner, the lapping ocean surrounding them. On Nico's instructions the bartender had brought two shot glasses and a bottle of vodka to their table.

Nico had poured them both a hefty measure and raised his glass. 'To Rosa Carty,' he had said with an approving nod.

'To me?'

'The most efficient PA in the western hemisphere.'

She had been flummoxed at the unexpected compliment. 'I just do my job.'

'And you do it superbly. I am the envy of my compatriots.'

Before she could respond her phone buzzed for the ninth time that evening.

'Who keeps messaging you?' he asked with a definite hint of irritation.

'My ex,' she muttered, firing a text back.

'Your ex? If he is an ex, why is he contacting you?'

'It's personal.'

He leant forward. 'We are off the clock now, Rosa. We are socializing, not preparing a board meeting. Tell me.'

They might be 'off the clock', as he so eloquently put it, but there was no mistaking a direct order. 'I changed the locks of my flat before coming to California. He's not very happy about it but I'm fed up with him turning up and letting himself in whenever he feels like it.'

A shadow crossed Nico's eyes. 'Has he threatened you?'

'Not in a physical sense. He's convinced that if he keeps the pressure up I'll go back to him.' She straightened her spine. 'But I won't. Sooner or later he'll get the message.'

'When did you end it?'

'Two months ago.'

'You'd have thought he'd have got the message by now.'

As if proving his point, her phone buzzed again.

Before she could open the message he reached over and removed the mobile from her hand.

'If you keep answering you'll only encourage him,' he said in a no-nonsense manner.

'If I don't answer he sends twice as many.' As she spoke Nico's smartphone beeped in turn.

He looked at the screen, then back at Rosa. 'How long were you with him?'

'Three years.'

He held his smartphone up. 'I enjoyed the grand total of two dates with Sophie before she started hinting at making things *permanent*.' His lips tightened. 'I ended it but she will not accept it. It is always the same. Women always want to make things permanent.'

'That's because you're such a catch,' she said, snatching her phone back. 'How old are you? Thirty-five?'

'Thirty-six,' he corrected.

She looked back down at her phone and read the latest pleading message. 'Well, then—they all think you're ready to settle down.'

'Not with one of them.' He downed his shot of vodka and then tapped the side of Rosa's full glass. 'Your turn. And if you don't turn your phone off I will throw it in the ocean.'

'Try it,' she said absently, her attention focused on the screen in front of her. She had tried everything to make Stephen get the message. Being nice. Being cruel. None of it was getting through to him.

Before her finger could even touch the keypad to form a response Nico took the phone out of her hand and threw it over the railing and into the ocean. It made a lovely splashing sound before disappearing into the dark water.

The anger that surged through her blood at this high-handed, outrageous act was as unexpected as the deed itself.

She stared at him in disbelief.

There was no contrition. He simply sat there with one brow raised, his features arranged into a perfect display of nonchalance.

She could never have known then that less than twelve hours later she would marry him.

But she *had* married him. And now she had to deal with the consequences.

Walking over to the long breakfast bar, grabbing her mug of coffee on the way, she hooked a stool out with her foot and took a seat. Her stomach was doing funny flipping motions and she could not take her eyes off the beautiful gift-wrapping. It must have taken him ages to get it so perfect.

It was not until she turned the gift upside down to unwrap it that she saw the sticker holding the ribbon to the box. She recognised the insignia on it and knew in an instant that it had been professionally gift-wrapped. She tried not to let dejection set in. So what if he hadn't wrapped it himself? He had thought of her.

Tearing it open, she found a bottle of expensive perfume.

Nico took the stool opposite and gazed at her expectantly. Black stubble had broken out on his chiselled jawline which, combined with his neatly trimmed goatee, gave him a slightly sinister yet wholly masculine air. His usually tousled black hair was even messier than usual. Rosa found herself fighting her own hands to stop herself from smoothing it down— an urge that had been increasing over recent months, and an urge that only served to prove that the course of action she was about to take was for the best.

She looked back at the gift. 'It's lovely. Thank you.' Then she made the mistake of turning it over in her hand and catching sight of the duty-free label on the bottom.

It brought to mind the old T-shirt she recalled one of her foster sisters continuously wearing: 'My dad went to Blackpool and all he brought me was this lousy T-shirt'. Most likely it was the only gift the child's father *had* brought her.

In Nico's case he had been to Morocco. And all he had brought her was some duty-free perfume. As a birthday present.

If she hadn't known how offended he would be she would have laughed. Although generous to a fault, Nico was simply not wired to lavish gifts on people. He hadn't even bought her a Christmas card—had been astonished to receive the gift of a silk tie and cufflinks from her.

She would bet none of his lovers had ever been kissed off with an expensive piece of jewellery. His brain did not work that way. The very fact that he had bought something for her touched her deeply, lodging a crumb of doubt into her certainty.

'So, what did you do for your birthday?' he asked as if he *hadn't* stood her up at the very last minute, as if she *hadn't* been all dressed up and waiting for him.

Since she had stopped working for him he had stood her up at the last minute a couple of times. She tried very hard to be philosophical about it—with his line of work, and the different time-zones he travelled between, it couldn't always be helped.

When she had worked for him they had spent around half their time abroad. Since she had left Baranski Mining three months ago they had shared a roof twenty-nine times. She had counted.

She had never been able to shake the feeling she was being punished for having the temerity to refuse his offer of a permanent role.

His failure to return home for her birthday had felt like having a twisting knife plunged into her heart.

'Stephen took me to La Torina.'

'Stephen?'

For the ghost of a second she could have sworn his sensuous lips tightened, that the pupils of his eyes pulsed. She blinked, certain she was imagining it, and found his features arranged in their usual indifference.

She nodded, challenging him, *willing* him to make something of it.

'Do I take it Stephen is the sender of the flowers on the reception table?'

'Yes. Aren't they beautiful?' She took a sip of her coffee and waited for some form of reaction from him.

'They certainly brighten the room up.' His tone was casual. They could be discussing a dull day at the office. 'Did you sleep with him?'

She didn't flinch or hesitate, simply held her chin aloft in silent defiance. 'Yes.'

Her stomach clenched as she gazed into the piercing green eyes of the man she had married. She searched intently, looking for a sign of *something*—some form of emotion, something to show he cared. But there was nothing to be found. There never had been. It shouldn't matter. After all, emotions had never been part of the deal between them.

Their marriage hadn't been all bad. For the most part it had been good—at least until she had left Baranski Mining. They had worked fantastically well together, both professionally and socially.

She remembered one evening when they had attended a charity auction and the auctioneer had had a large dollop of cream stuck to his ear. She and Nico had sat there like robots, not daring to look at each other, the corners of their mouths twitching with mirth. It hadn't meant anything, but it had been one of those rare moments when she had felt perfect alignment with him.

It was a moment of togetherness, and they had become few and far between.

And it *did* matter.

His indifference hurt more every time she looked at it.

'I would say good for you,' he said, studying her closely. 'It is time you took a lover. But there is something ironic about you falling into bed with the man you married me to escape from.'

The irony had not been lost on her either.

If Stephen had called ten minutes earlier the outcome would have been very different.

She had just come off the phone to Nico, and he had given her a brusque explanation of why he wouldn't make it back in time to take her out for her birthday.

She'd been all dressed up with nowhere to go.

And she'd made the mistake of reading her brother's text message for possibly the hundredth time.

It had been one of the lowest points of her life.

Then Stephen had called to wish her a happy birthday. If she hadn't felt so heartsick she would have hung the receiver up. Instead she had found herself agreeing to a meal.

Company. That was what she'd craved. Freddy Krueger could have offered her a date and she would have accepted.

'Nico, I—'

'Let us pause this conversation for a minute,' he interrupted, getting to his feet. 'It has been a long day. I could use a proper drink and something comfortable to sit on.'

A drink sounded good to her. Lord knew she needed something to numb the curdling of her belly. Because, for all the seeming indifference of his words, Nico's powerful body was taut with tension, like a coil waiting to spring free.

She followed him through to the spacious living room and curled up on the sofa while he poured them both a hefty measure of vodka.

It was certainly a day for irony. Vodka had played its part in the start of their marriage and now it would play its part in its demise. She took a long sip, welcoming the numbing burn of the clear liquid, before placing it on the coffee table.

She waited until he had settled in the sofa opposite before speaking. Her words came out in a rush. 'Nico, this isn't working.'

'What isn't working?'

'This.' She threw her arms in the air and gave a rueful shrug. 'Us. Our marriage. I want out.'

CHAPTER TWO

Rosa was unnerved by Nico's stillness. He leant forward, his muscular forearms resting on his thighs, his glass cradled between his large hands. 'Are you getting back together with Stephen?'

'No…'

His eyes did not leave her face. 'You left him because he suffocated you.'

'I'm not getting back with Stephen.'

'He wouldn't take no for an answer,' he continued. 'You were on the verge of getting a restraining order against him when you married me.'

'I know.' She expelled stale air through her teeth and closed her eyes. She had no wish to explain the utter desperation she had felt on her birthday, the horrendous feeling that there was not a soul in the world who cared if she lived or died. 'Sleeping with him was a mistake that will not be repeated.' A huge mistake. A massive mistake of epic proportions. But it did have one advantage—it had allowed her to see the enormous error she had made marrying Nico.

'Is there someone else?'

'No. There is no one else.' How could there be?

'Then why do you want to leave?'

She wished he wouldn't look at her with such menacing stillness. Nico always kept his cards close to his chest, but she couldn't help feeling as if he were trying to penetrate through to her brain and dissect the contents. If only she had the slightest clue as to what he was thinking.

'Because it isn't working for me any more.' She reached for a squishy cushion and cuddled it to her belly, hoping the comfort would quell the butterflies raging inside. 'We agreed from the start that if either of us wanted to leave we could, without any fuss. Nico, I want a fresh start. I want a divorce.'

Nico remained still as he stared hard at the woman he had married, his eyes flickering down to the gold band she wore on her finger. A ring *he* had put there.

'I am well aware of what we agreed, Rosa. However, it is unreasonable for you to suddenly state you want a divorce and not give me a valid reason.'

'There is no single valid reason.' She tugged a stray lock of her ebony hair behind her ear. 'When we agreed to marry it seemed the perfect solution for both of us—a nice, convenient open marriage. No emotional ties or anything messy...' Her husky voice trailed off. 'I don't know exactly what I want from a marriage—I don't know if I even want a marriage— but, Nicolai, I do know I want something more than this.'

It was the use of his full first name that convinced him she was serious. She had addressed him by his shortened name since they'd exchanged their wedding vows. That, and the fact they were speaking in English.

Rosa adored the Russian tongue. They rarely spoke her native language when together.

His hands tightened around his glass and he took a long sip of the clear, fiery liquid. Rosa was a lot like vodka. Clear and pure-looking, but with a definite bite. In her own understated way she did not take crap from anyone.

He pursed his lips as he contemplated her, sitting there,

studying him with an openness he had always admired. He had admired her from the start.

After his PA had gone into early labour he'd had no choice but to approach an employment agency to fill the role. There had been no one in his employ suitable for it.

The agency had duly sent six candidates—all of whom, they'd assured him, were fluent in Russian. By the time he had interviewed the first five he'd been ready to sue the agency. The candidates had been useless. Never mind that their Russian had been far from fluent, he doubted they could have organised a children's party.

And then in had walked Rosa Carty, the model of calm efficiency.

Her Russian was flawless. Perfect. He would trust her to organise a state funeral.

He had offered her the position immediately and she had started on the hoof, with no training or guidance. She had stepped into the breach as if she had always been there.

She had never flirted with him, had never dressed as anything but the professional she was, had never brought her private life to the office. She had been perfect.

Marriage had always been an institution he admired but one he had long accepted would not be for him.

Five months on and he had been in his office with Serge, his finance director and an old friend from his university days. They had been going over the figures for his buyout of a Californian mine when there had been a sharp rap at the door and Rosa had walked in.

He had known immediately something was wrong. She would never have dreamt of interrupting a meeting unless it was important.

'We have a slight problem,' she had said in her usual understated fashion. 'There is a discrepancy with the output figures.'

She had lain the offending document before him and pointed to a tiny section highlighted in pink. The figure in question had been out by less than an eighth of one per cent, but in financial terms equated to over a million pounds.

At least ten pairs of eyes, including his own, had gone through the document. Rosa was the only person to have picked up on the error.

After agreeing on an action plan, she had set off to implement it. He'd had no doubt the whole thing would be rectified by the end of the day.

'Your PA is really something,' Serge had said with a shake of his head when she'd left the office. 'When Madeline comes back from maternity leave can I have Rosa in my department?'

Nico had shrugged noncommittally. Even at that stage he had known he wanted to keep Rosa as his PA—had been busy strategising ways to keep her working directly for him without landing himself with a lawsuit from a disgruntled Madeline.

'Is she married?' Serge had asked with a sudden knowing look in his eyes. 'She is exactly the kind of woman a man like you should marry.'

If Serge hadn't been one of his oldest friends Nico would have fired him on the spot for insubordination.

'There is nothing worse than a newly married man,' he said drily.

'Marriage has been the making of me,' Serge countered amiably. 'Seriously, my friend, Rosa would be perfect for you. She's got the same coolness as you. You have mentioned breaking into the Middle East. Socialising is a big part of their business culture and marriage is very much respected. Rosa would be an asset to you. Besides,' he continued with a flash of his teeth, 'a man can't stay happy all his life!'

Days later he had travelled to California with Rosa and

an army of workers. As the days passed, Serge's words had kept repeating in his head.

By their last day he had almost convinced himself that his friend could be on to something.

He had engineered things so that he and Rosa were alone after the celebratory meal, sitting in the balmy night air, drinking vodka. Usually his employees' private lives and private time were strictly off-limits, but that night he had wanted to test if their compatibility in the office could be matched in a social setting.

The constant buzz of her phone had driven him to distraction. Well, it had been more the fact that she'd kept ignoring him to answer those annoying messages that had irritated him. And the fact that he'd disliked her responding to someone who was so clearly deranged. So he'd thrown her phone into the ocean.

She had simply glared at him, a small tick playing under her left eye. 'That was unnecessary.'

'Every time you respond you give him false hope,' he pointed out. 'The only way to be rid of him is to cut all communication. I will replace your phone. Now, drink your shot.'

For the breadth of a moment he thought she would throw the glass at him.

Instead she lifted the shot and downed it. In one. Done, she slammed the glass back on the table and eyeballed him with caramel eyes that swirled with amusement. 'There. Happy now?'

A bubble of laughter climbed his throat. He had never imagined his starchy, temporary PA possessed a personality.

'So you never contemplated marrying…?'

'Stephen,' she supplied with a hiccup. She put her hand to her mouth and threw him a wry smile. 'No. Never in a million years would I have married him. Although I'd love to marry *someone*, right now, just to get him off my back.' She shook her head. 'I do like the idea of marriage, but I'd be a rubbish wife. I'm married to my work and I much prefer my own company.'

Nico nodded, understanding. 'I like the idea of a wife who can accompany me to functions and hold an intelligent conversation.' He chose his words carefully. 'But the thought of all that *emoting* couples are supposed to do leaves me cold.'

'Tell me about it,' she agreed with pursed lips.

He looked, at her—*really* looked at her. Serge's assessment had been right. Rosa would be an asset to any businessman. And *he* would be that businessman.

She could be a female version of him! Both were perfectionists. Both were dedicated to their work. Nico had long wanted marriage for the respectability it afforded, but after Galina—his one heavy entanglement and the only failure in his life—he had known he was not cut out for relationships. He was not made that way.

'We could marry,' he said idly, watching closely for her reaction.

The vodka Rosa had just poured into her mouth was spat out.

'Think about it,' he said, warming to his theme. 'We would be perfect together.'

'Yes,' she said, pulling a face once she had finished choking. 'And all those socialites would have to stop harassing you for marriage.'

'More importantly, from your perspective, Stephen would get the picture that you are never coming back. But that's neither here nor there. You are a woman of great intellect. We work well together. There is no reason we could not have a successful marriage.'

'This all sounds fabulous,' she said, with a roll of her eyes. 'But there are a couple of slight problems.'

'Which are?'

'One: we don't fancy each other.'

Even Nico was vain enough to bristle slightly at that remark. 'That means there is no chance of us falling into bed and messing things up by letting emotions get in the way.' Although, looking at her, he had to admit there was something appealing about her in a fresh-faced, pretty kind of way. Not that he would ever be tempted to do anything about it. No. Rosa was not his type at all.

'Two.' She ticked the number off on her fingers. 'I don't believe in mixing business with pleasure.'

'Neither do I. But as this is a business proposal that would not be a problem.'

Her eyes suddenly widened. 'My God, are you serious?'

'Absolutely. Think about it, Rosa. We would be perfect together. We both want marriage…'

'Just not to anyone who would expect us to compromise our lives for it,' she finished with an unexpected sparkle.

'This calls for a drink.' He poured them both another hefty measure of vodka and chinked his glass to hers. On the count of three they downed them.

Done, Nico reached for his smartphone and started a search.

'We can marry here, tonight, in California,' he said, reading quickly. 'As long as we've got our passports, we're good to go.'

'Excellent.' She pulled her briefcase onto her lap and rummaged through it.

'What are you doing?'

'Looking for a pen and some paper.'

'What for?'

She had looked at him, amusement written all over her face. 'If we're going to get married it's only right we make a contract for it. Shall I write it in English or Russian?'

And that had been it. They had married, still slightly tipsy, the next morning.

Not once had he been given cause to regret their impulsive decision—the only impulsive decision he had made in his thirty-six years.

And now she had the nerve to sit there, eleven months on, and tell him she had *changed her mind.*

Not only that, but she had slept with her ex.

A wave of nausea rolled through his stomach—so violent he almost retched.

He was in no position to complain. He should be able to accept that. They had made an agreement that theirs would be an open marriage. As long as they exercised discretion they could sleep with whomever they chose.

Was he not a modern, twenty-first-century man? He had no right to feel possessive about a woman who was his wife in name only.

Intellectually, he knew all the right things to think.

Under the surface of his skin, though, his latent Neanderthal had reared up and punched him hard, right in the solar plexus.

She had slept with someone else. That little gem had lodged in his chest and was piercing into him with regular stabbing motions.

She had slept with someone else and had the nerve to think that *she* could call the shots.

He had bought her a birthday present. The first personal gift he had ever bought a woman. *And she had slept with someone else.*

Had she slept with her ex as punishment for him not returning in time for her birthday? With any other woman the answer would be a resounding yes. But Rosa was not made in the same mould as other women. Or so he had thought.

'You should have told me you were unhappy.' As he spoke,

something rancid nibbled away at his gut—which he tried to quash with another sip of his vodka.

She threw him a wan smile. 'I'm not unhappy—more lonely, I guess.'

'That would not have been a problem if you had taken the job permanently when I offered it to you.'

It was an issue that still rankled. A week before Madeline, his original PA, had been due to return from maternity leave, she had dropped the bombshell that she would not be coming back. He'd hidden his delight, wished her well, and promptly offered the job to his wife.

She had refused to take it. She'd turned his generous offer down, just as she'd refused all subsequent offers of employment within the Baranski Mining empire.

Ever since he had accrued enough money to purchase Reuben Mining and turn it into Baranski Mining no one had ever refused him anything.

'Nico, I was lonely when I worked for you.'

How was that even possible? They had spent nearly every waking hour together.

He took another long sip of his vodka. 'I do hope this decision will not affect our trip to Butterfly Island,' he said, struggling to keep an even tone. He must be more exhausted than he had appreciated, because his mood was darkening as rapidly as his musings. And the rolls of nausea were increasing.

She sighed and pulled out the band holding her ponytail, before immediately gathering all the stray locks and tying it up again, stretching her creamy skin taut.

He preferred it when she wore her silky black tresses loose, as she did on the occasions when they accompanied each other to social functions. With her hair loose, her angular features softened, her caramel eyes, under which purple smudges currently resided, became rounder.

'We are due to fly there in a fortnight,' he reminded her tightly. 'We had an agreement and I expect you to honour it.'

The new PA he had appointed three months ago, when Rosa had refused the job, had proved herself to be spectacularly useless. And the one he had hired after sacking that one. And the next. As he had found since Rosa had moved on, when compared with his wife's calm, dedicated efficiency, they were all useless.

Rosa's eyes widened a fraction. 'You *expect*?' she questioned in that husky voice he usually found so soothing.

'Yes. A commitment is a commitment. Like our marriage.'

Dimly he recalled a conversation one evening about how his plans for mineral mining in the Indian Ocean were firming up. He was readying for the contractual stage now, which meant he would need a Russian-speaking assistant to accompany him to Butterfly Island for the contract completion. He remembered complaining of the impossibility of finding someone and training them up in time, which was when Rosa had offered to accompany him instead. Just as he had hoped she would. She had landed a job working as a translator for another London-based Russian firm, but was willing to use her holiday entitlement to assist him.

'I know.' Her nose wrinkled. She gave a little shiver and rubbed her arms, pushing her full breasts together; unaware that the late-afternoon sunlight filtering in through the big bay window illuminated her white T-shirt, making it virtually transparent.

He averted his eyes and willed away the tingles of awareness spreading through him.

What the hell was the matter with him? His wife had told him she'd slept with her ex and wanted a divorce, and his body was *still* capable of reacting to her?

Although she was not his type, intellectually he was aware

that Rosa was an attractive woman. That awareness had been growing in recent months. There had even been times when...

No. He had never allowed the idea of anything physical between them to take root. If it had been anyone but Rosa he would not have thought twice about acting on it, but he had never been able to shake the feeling that sleeping with her would be akin to opening a can of worms.

Maybe he should have done.

'I would be grateful if you could take someone else in my place.'

Her words cut through his inappropriate meanderings.

'Impossible. It is far too short notice.'

She arched an eyebrow. 'Rubbish. You employ plenty of linguists of both nationalities.'

He fought to keep his tone even. 'But none as good as you—as you well know. And even if I could find and train someone at such short notice, it is *you* I want.'

'Really?'

The inflection in her tone made him pause. Somehow he didn't think she was referring to work.

'I'm sorry, Nico, but it's out of the question. I know it is an inconvenience, but two weeks is by no means too short notice.'

Two weeks to find another Rosa was impossible.

'I've been looking on the internet and we can sort the divorce out ourselves.'

'What are you talking about?'

'Our divorce,' she said evenly. 'There's no point in us appointing lawyers. I don't want anything from you, and unless you want something from me—'

'I don't recall agreeing to any divorce,' he cut in, the grip on his glass tightening.

She had it all figured out. She seriously thought she could

tell him she wanted a divorce and then waltz off into the moonlight.

The nausea rolled up into his throat and lodged there, burning his vocal cords.

She seriously thought he would let her go.

Her warm eyes chilled and narrowed. 'Actually, you did. When we married. Remember?'

He forced his throat to work. 'That was eleven months ago. My feelings on the matter have changed.' Hell could freeze over before he let her leave.

'Well, mine haven't. As far as I'm concerned, my feelings on divorce are the same as they were then.' She got to her feet and stood as tall as her short, curvy frame would allow. 'I'm sorry if my decision somehow inconveniences you—I had assumed you wouldn't be bothered—and I'm sorry if somehow I have disappointed you, but, Nicolai, I can't stay in this sham of a marriage for a second longer.'

Sadness rang in her eyes before she turned and headed for the door.

'Where do you think you're going?'

Her spine became rigid. 'To collect my belongings. I packed earlier.'

'And where do you intend to go? To *Stephen*?'

As he spoke her lover's name the glass in his hand shattered.

CHAPTER THREE

Rosa vacuumed the last tiny shard of glass from the thick carpet.

Her hands had finally stopped shaking, but her heart still thundered painfully against her ribs.

Nico's face...

When that glass had shattered there had been a moment when she had thought his face would crack too.

Other than the usual business talk, it seemed he had barely noticed her existence in months. He might not have cared that she had slept with someone else, but she had been a fool to hope he would give her a divorce without putting up a fight.

She should have known better. If there was one thing she knew about her husband it was that he did not like to lose. At anything.

She had known Butterfly Island would be a problem—after all, he seemed to spend the majority of their limited time together bitching about the latest unfortunate to be appointed the role of his PA—but she had put that down to his being miffed that she had refused the job. Her husband's success and power had put him in the unfortunate position of seldom being denied anything he wanted. He had not taken her refusal to continue working for him well—had taken it as a personal slight. Which, of course, it had been—but not in the way he assumed.

By the time her contract with Baranski Mining had expired Rosa's feelings towards him had become far too complicated for her even to consider staying on. She had fervently hoped some distance from him would settle the weird hormones unleashed by their working so closely together. It hadn't worked. She had been left rattling round their huge home alone while he travelled the globe, rarely spending more than a couple of nights in London at any one time.

She had missed him. God help her, she had missed him.

She was wedging the vacuum back in the cupboard when Nico came out of the downstairs bathroom, where he had been washing shards of glass off his hand. Somehow the shattered glass hadn't even nicked him. The man must be made of Teflon.

She had no idea what he had done to his hair, but even taking into account its usual messiness it was sticking up as if he'd rubbed a balloon on it.

For some reason this tugged at her.

The cool façade had definitely cracked.

His features were arranged in their usual indifference, but the pulse in his jaw was working double-time. This was the closest to angry she had ever seen him.

Closing the cupboard, she took a deep breath. 'In answer to your question, I'm going to stay at a hotel until the lease on my flat expires.' Thank God she'd had the foresight to grant her tenants only a short-term lease. She missed her cosy flat dreadfully. But at least in a hotel she wouldn't be alone, and in the meantime she could start hunting for a new flatmate to share with.

If there was one thing she hated it was living alone. Marrying Nico had, at the time, been a godsend. With Stephen gone, she had been trying to find a flatmate—someone who was happy to share a home with her without wanting to spend every evening drinking wine and having girly chats.

Nico's mad idea had been the answer to every prayer she'd had. He wouldn't expect anything from her other than intellectual stimulation. In return she would have his name and a ring on her finger. Symbols that she belonged to someone. And he wore *her* ring. A metaphorical symbol that he belonged to her too.

'I think not.' His green eyes had darkened into an almost sinister gleam. 'You see, Rosa, under no circumstances will I allow you to leave. I do not want a divorce. Go up to your room and unpack—you're not going anywhere.'

Rosa reared back and stared at him. Surely he hadn't just said what she thought he had? 'You won't *allow* me to leave?'

His mouth formed a thin, grim line. 'You are my wife.'

'Exactly. I am your wife—not your possession.'

'In certain cultures that is one and the same thing.'

'Well, luckily for me we're in the UK, and not some backwards country where women have no voice.'

'I will never agree to a divorce.'

She studied him carefully, half expecting him to crack a smile and say he was joking. Surely he could not be serious? However, she did have one more ace up her sleeve—no one could ever accuse her of being anything but thorough. 'If you won't agree to a divorce I will apply for an annulment. This marriage was never consummated. Therefore it is void.'

Not bothering to wait for a response, Rosa walked away. Determined to keep a cool head, she walked steadily up the stairs to her suite, placing a hand to her chest in a futile attempt to temper her thundering heart.

Thankfully she'd had the foresight to pack earlier—a job that had taken less than an hour.

Heavy footsteps neared her and mentally she braced herself.

Nico crossed the threshold into her bedroom, his features so taut he might have been carved from ice. His eyes, though… His eyes shimmered with fury.

'You do realise you can't stop me?' she said coldly.

He folded his arms across his chest, accentuating the breadth of his physique. Nico really was a mountain of a man, filling the space around him, dwarfing everything in the vicinity. 'I think you'll find I can.'

'By using force?' She didn't believe he would do that. Not for a second. He might be over a foot taller than her, and packed full of solid muscle, but she knew perfectly well he would never use that to his advantage.

His lips curved into a cold smile. 'I don't need to use physical force, Rosa. I have other advantages to stop you leaving.'

'Why are you being like this?' She forced her voice to remain calm. 'Why can't you just accept I want out?'

'I'll tell you why,' he said, stalking towards her, his eyes glittering. 'You see, *daragaya*, I have just learned that not only have I been cuckolded but, to add insult to injury, you want to humiliate me too.'

It was the casual, almost sneering way he called her *his darling wife* that did it. Something inside of her snapped. Gazing up at him, mere feet away, close enough for her to feel the heat emanating from his powerful body, she said, 'Cuckolded? Humiliated? What planet are you on? How many women have you slept with since we married?'

Oh, he had been discreet. She would give him that. But there was no way a man as overtly masculine as Nico would go eleven months without sex.

'Do not try to twist the subject. We are not talking about me. We are talking about you and the fact you want to advertise to the world that we never have consummated our marriage.'

'You know damn well I won't be doing anything of the sort.'

'You think the press won't leap on a nugget like that? You think I want to be the butt of everyone's gossip? To know friends and business acquaintances will speculate over the reasons you and I never had sex?'

Rosa turned her face away, a slow burn crawling up her neck.

Lord, she did not want to *think* of them having sex. It was bad enough dreaming about his hard, naked body taking her passionately and then waking up in the morning with a burning need deep inside her, knowing there was nothing she could do about it other than take as cold a shower as she could bear and push it from her mind. At least she could control her conscious thoughts.

She took a step away from him—away from that citrusy, masculine scent that was starting to swirl around her senses. 'I don't relish that scenario any more than you, but if you refuse a divorce you will leave me no other option than to go down the annulment road.'

'I will deny it,' he said, staring at her unsmilingly. 'I will tell the courts that you are a fantasist.'

'You would lie under oath?'

The ring of shock in Rosa's eyes was all too apparent.

In truth, Nico had shocked himself.

Would he really go that far? Under ordinary circumstances the answer would be a resounding no. But these were far from ordinary circumstances.

Her suitcases sat neatly by her bedroom door. A sign of her intent.

Of her defiance.

Without any pause for thought, he reached for the nearest, flicked the clips to spring it open and tipped the contents into a heap on the floor.

'I will do whatever is necessary to uphold my reputation,'

he said, staring intently into her startled eyes. He clenched his hands into fists and held them tightly by his sides to prevent them doing the same to the other suitcase. He had made his point. 'You are a Baranski and will remain a Baranski for as long as I deem necessary.'

Rosa backed away from him like a wary cat, tugging at her ponytail, loathing written all over her pretty face. 'I'll be a Carty again before you can blink,' she said, her chest rising up and down with rapid motion. 'I'll change my name back by deed poll if necessary. And if you think upending my possessions is going to make me stay, then you are delusional.'

He would never have guessed his starchy wife was capable of anger. Irritation, yes. Mild annoyance on a bad day, maybe. But full-blown anger? No.

She had not even raised her voice but he could feel it—those tiny ripples of fury kept under the tightest of reins.

What would it be like to unleash that passion? A passion he had blithely ignored over the eleven months of their marriage, not even aware of its existence.

It had been there all along. And another man had been the recipient of it.

The knowledge lingered in his senses like a pungent smell.

And it made him react in ways he had never believed himself capable of.

'I have a proposition for you,' he said, breaking the taut silence.

Her eyes narrowed in suspicion.

'I do not want a divorce or an annulment. I like our marriage—it suits me very well.' And he was damned if he was going to let it end on her terms. If they were going to divorce it would be on *his* terms and his terms only.

'It doesn't suit *me*.'

Clamping down on the fresh flash of rage that followed this little declaration, he forced his voice to remain calm. 'I realise that. However, as you have done so much research you must be aware that we cannot divorce until we have been married for a year—which in our case is a whole month away.'

'That doesn't mean we can't start the ball rolling,' she said, displaying the stubbornness he had always admired in her when she had worked for him, working regular twelve hour days in an effort to ensure everything was in perfect order.

It was the same stubbornness she had displayed when she'd refused his every overture to work with him permanently.

With a flash of insight he realised the more he tried to force her to comply the more she would dig her heels in. Her obstinancy was liable to take the form of an immovable object.

Why had he never noticed how sexy such stubbornness could be?

He squashed the thought away.

'Give me a month—until the date of our first anniversary—to change your mind,' he said, in the most reasonable voice he could muster. 'Come to Butterfly Island with me as planned—you're a first-class PA and linguist, and there is no one capable of doing the job as well as you. Do that and I will grant you a divorce. Refuse, and I will fight you every inch of the way.'

'I won't change my mind.'

'That remains to be seen. But unless you give me the next month to try you will find yourself with one almighty fight on your hands.' Deliberately he stepped towards her, over the puddle of clothes, encroaching on her personal space— a move he had never made in all the time he had known her. 'I will contest it every step of the way. If I wanted, I could play dirty and drag it on for years. And guess what? I never lose.'

A small tick pounded under her left eye, so tiny it was barely perceptible. He had only seen that particular affliction once before. Smelling victory, he pressed on a little further, leaning close enough to smell her clean, feminine scent. He swallowed the moisture that formed in his mouth.

'One month, Rosa. I don't think that's a very long time to wait for a lifetime of freedom.'

She gazed back at him, the tiny tick still pounding, before she visibly hardened. 'I want it in writing.'

'I beg your pardon?' His lips curled. He had never been so insulted. 'I am giving you my word.'

'You gave me your word eleven months ago.'

'And you gave me yours. I am not the one planning to break my vows.'

For an age they simply stared at each other, neither bending. The tension between them had become so thick a steak knife would have had trouble cutting through it. Yet through the seeping tension he could not help but admire her. There were not many people brave enough to face him off.

Rosa caved in first. Extending her hand, she said, 'We will shake on it. One month, Nicolai. And if at the end you refuse to give me my divorce then I will show you just how dirty *I* can play.'

Her fiery declaration sent a frisson of excitement racing through his veins. As he reached for her hand he realised it was the first time their flesh had touched since they had exchanged their rings.

And as he walked back down the stairs, victory still ringing within him, Nico realised it had also been the first time he had set foot in her suite since she had moved in.

A black Jeep awaited them at the landing strip that constituted Butterfly Island's airport.

It was roasting hot, the heat shimmering like waves off the ground. Even though Rosa had had the foresight to change into a light, cotton summer dress, her skin was dampening by the second.

It had been eighteen hours since they'd left London and she was shattered. The thirteen hour flight on Nico's plush private jet hadn't been too bad, but she had been far too wired to sleep. Unlike Nico, who had the amazing knack of being able to sleep on command.

Fortunately she'd had a pile of documents to read through to keep her occupied. She'd devoted all her spare time over the past fortnight in getting up to speed on the contracts. There had been little else for her to do. Nico had been as elusive over the past two weeks as an escaped hamster.

The one-hour connecting flight to Butterfly Island on a four-seat Cessna had been a more cramped affair. Nico had sat in front of her. They had been close enough to touch— close enough for her to smell him.

She had spent the flight breathing through her mouth.

A squat, elderly gentleman who looked dressed for a safari, in a cream pocketed shirt, cream shorts, a panama hat and long white socks, got out of the Jeep and strode over to them. For his part, Nico had relaxed his strict business attire by removing his jacket and tie and rolling up his sleeves.

'Nicolai—as always, it's a pleasure to have your company.'

'Likewise.' Nico shook the offered hand vigorously. 'Allow me to introduce you to my wife, Rosa. Rosa, this is Robert King—owner of Butterfly Island and King Island.'

His wife? Nico had introduced her as his *wife*? In the eight months she had continued working for him after their quickie wedding he had never introduced her as anything other than his assistant. They had agreed that when it came to business it was best to keep things on a professional footing.

Before she could think about this in any depth she was pulled into the American's arms. 'Wonderful to meet you, Rosa. Your husband has told me all about you.' He released her, but kept hold of her forearms so he could look at her. 'Nicolai, you never told me what a beauty she was.'

Nico placed an arm around her waist in what could only be described as a possessive manner, forcing a reluctant Robert to release her. Rosa, already reeling at being called a *beauty*, was so shocked at this unexpected and blatant show of possessiveness that she froze.

'Rosa's beauty speaks for itself,' said Nico in his gravelly tones. 'Now, have all the arrangements been made?'

She was not sure if she'd imagined it, but she could have sworn Robert dropped him a quick wink. 'Everything's in hand.'

The minor stupor caused by Nico's introduction and his unprecedented hold on her receded, and she extracted herself from his arm. 'It's wonderful to meet you too, Mr King, but—as I'm sure *my husband* has already informed you—I have accompanied him as his assistant and not his wife.'

'His assistant, eh?' Robert's wink was a lot more obvious this time. 'I get you, I get you. Say no more. Now, you folks must be exhausted after all that travelling. Let's get you to your accommodation so you can freshen up. Oh—and, Rosa? It's Robert.'

The air-conditioning in the Jeep had been turned to full blast. Rosa welcomed the freshness after the stifling heat of the airstrip. It was the only thing she did welcome as the men started to talk business. Robert didn't exactly freeze her out of the conversation but all his attention was focused on Nico. She had a feeling if she offered an opinion he would ruffle her hair and tell her not to worry her pretty head about it. It was infuriating, but not half as infuriating as Nico's obliviousness to it.

She comforted herself with the knowledge that once Robert had seen her work he would see for himself that she was there *not* out of the virtue of being Nico's wife but out of the virtue of being good at her job.

Still, it made for an uncomfortable journey—at least for her.

Butterfly Island was small by anyone's standards. According to her research, its circumference was only a touch over nine miles. They reached the complex where they were to stay for the next fortnight in less than ten minutes.

To Rosa's eyes it certainly lived up to its high-class honeymoon resort billing. When over the past fortnight she'd allowed herself to think of being in a lovers' paradise with the man who was her husband but not her lover, she had consoled herself that she would be too busy working to have time to witness any open signs of affection displayed by the other guests.

The driver pulled up outside a large, one-storey Tuscan-style villa.

'I'll leave you two to settle in.' Robert grinned, throwing her a wink. 'Get a good night's sleep and I'll get a golf-buggy to collect you after breakfast and bring you to the hotel. The conference room's all ready to go. And, Rosa—' he winked at her again '—the spa here has been named one of the best in the world. My staff have all been instructed to give you preferential treatment on anything you desire.'

'That is very kind. I'll be sure to remember that.' She smiled. The shimmering heat of the day and the ambient atmosphere of the island had already started working its magic on her. What was the point in getting antsy? He was an old man. She would change his mind soon enough. 'See you in the morning.'

Entering the villa, she tightened her ponytail and sighed with pleasure.

'Shall I take your luggage to your bedroom?' the driver asked, depositing their cases on the terracotta floor.

'I shall deal with it,' Nico said, slipping him some local currency.

Once they were alone, he turned to Rosa. 'I need to check in with the Moscow office, so take a look around.'

Leaving him to it, she headed off into the open-plan living quarters, which were as airy and sophisticated as one would expect for a villa of this calibre. On the gleaming dining table stood a bucket of champagne on ice, a large bowl of fresh fruit and a vase of the prettiest, most delicious-smelling flowers she had ever seen or sniffed. Tucked away discreetly in a corner to the rear was a large, fully equipped office, which she gave a cursory once-over before heading to the patio doors. Inspecting the office could wait. She would spend the next fortnight virtually chained to the desk.

She stepped out onto the decking. A sprawling lawn ran down to a sandy-white beach.

Bubbles of excitement started thrumming through her veins. Dozens of co-mingling scents converged under her nose, from fragrant flowers and freshly cut grass to the salty scent of the sea.

Rosa closed her eyes. She had travelled to many countries with Nico during her time as his PA. Relaxation had never been on the agenda. This trip would be no different. She was here to work.

All the same...

They'd always stayed in luxurious accommodation, but it had always been functional rather than beautiful.

Butterfly Island was stunning. This villa was stunning.

Wistfulness clutched at her belly. What would it be like if she were here with a lover? Someone she trusted enough to place her heart in his hands, who would not squeeze all the life out of it?

She scrubbed the image away—especially the image of Nico that kept trying to intrude. Finding another lover was the last thing on her mind. Sleeping with Stephen had been an act of folly—an act of desperation to purge the hurt that had almost consumed her whole.

CHAPTER FOUR

AFTER ONE LAST longing gaze at the beach, Rosa went back inside to search for the bedrooms. The first was easy to find, and immediately she chose it for herself. The bedroom, large and opulent, would be any honeymooner's dream. Its raised emperor four-poster bed even had the clichéd rose petals scattered all over the silk sheets. The *en suite* bathroom was *amazing*. The bath! She had never seen anything like it: sunken, with gold taps around the edges, it was large enough to swim in.

To stake her claim, she chucked her handbag on the bed and then left it to find Nico's bedroom.

A few minutes later, her brief good mood having plummeted, she found Nico in the partitioned office, his laptop open, still talking on his smartphone.

He took one look at her face and disconnected the call.

'What is wrong?' he asked. 'You look as if someone has stolen your luggage.'

She stood before him. 'There's only one bedroom.'

She waited for his disapproval.

He leaned back in the Captain's chair and stretched out his long legs. 'Naturally there is only one room.'

'What do you mean, "naturally"? I was assured by Camilla, or Emily, or whoever it is that currently runs your

London office, that a two-bedroomed villa had been reserved for us.'

'I changed it.'

Her chin nearly hit the floor. 'Why did you do that?'

'Because we are married, and married couples rarely sleep in separate beds. Unless, of course, they are not sharing conjugal relations.'

She shook her head slowly, wishing she could slap the smug arrogance off his face. 'You clever bastard.'

'I shall take that as a compliment.'

'It wasn't meant to be.' She knew exactly what he was playing at. 'I'm not sharing a bed with you. I assume it is enough that people *think* we are sleeping together?'

He shrugged nonchalantly. 'I do not control how other people think.'

'You'll have to sleep on the sofa.'

'I think not. I will be sleeping on that big, comfortable bed. If you wish to join me...?' He raised an eyebrow in invitation.

She blinked in shock.

Had that really been a suggestive tone in his voice? Surely not...

Unnerved, she took a step back.

Nico sat up and rested his forearms on his thighs, openly studying her. 'Does the thought of sharing a bed with me scare you?'

'Of course not,' she lied, inching back a little further—as far as the edge of the desk. He was still too close, but there was no way she was going to scurry off like a frightened rabbit just because he was close enough for her to smell his fruity scent.

They had worked side-by-side for the best part of a year and his scent had hardly ever been a problem for her—at least not until the last few months of her tenure. That had been one of the reasons she had turned down his offer of a permanent position. Nico smelled far too good for her sensibility.

'Then what is your problem?' His eyes gave a sudden gleam. 'Worried I won't be able to keep my hands off you?'

'Don't be ridiculous.' As if Nico had *ever* looked at her with anything other than platonic eyes.

'Why would you think that ridiculous? You're an attractive woman—sharing a bed with you would be a temptation for any man.'

To her horror, she felt her neck burn. She turned her head, unable to look at him, suddenly scared of what he would see. 'Now you *are* being ridiculous.'

His voice dropped to a murmur. 'I've thought about you a lot these past few weeks.'

She fixed her gaze on a pretty landscape painting on the wall. 'Sure you have.'

He had the audacity to laugh, with a low, gravelly timbre that sent tiny tingles dancing on her skin.

'You are angry with me for not spending any time with you. That would have been easily rectified if you were still working for me. You would have travelled with me.'

'Your ego astounds me.' She paused to swallow a lump that had formed in her throat. 'However, if your idea of getting me to change my mind about our marriage was to leave me alone for a fortnight, it was one heck of a rubbish plan.'

'I had matters to arrange and business to tie up before this trip.' He leaned closer and cupped the curve of her neck. 'Did you miss me?'

His unexpected action caught her off-guard. She would not have been more surprised if he had told her he was gay. She could understand the arm around her waist when they had been with Robert—Nico was doing all in his power to set her up to look a liar and a fool if she went down the annulment route—but *this*?

She had to fight with everything she had not to respond to the feel of his warm palm against her sensitised skin. She would *not* fall into his blatant trap.

'No.' She pulled away from his clasp—his second touch in less than an hour. 'I didn't miss you. Now, will you stop playing games? It's making me uncomfortable.'

His lips curved slightly. 'I am not playing games.'

'That's what it feels like.'

'You agreed to give me the chance to prove our marriage deserves another shot.'

'So far you have failed spectacularly. And pretending you find me attractive is not the way to go about it either.' Not after eleven months of complete uninterest.

'Have you considered that maybe I am not acting?'

The breath caught in her throat. If she hadn't already known how indifferent he was to her physically, she might almost have believed him.

She dragged air into her lungs and took a step to the side. 'Actually, no. I don't believe that for a second. You don't find me attractive. You're just using your masculinity to try and drive me into some kind of feminine stupor. You think I will fall for your charms and thus save you the unpleasantness of a public divorce—and save you from the hundreds of women who will come beating on your door, begging to be the new Mrs Baranski.'

He stilled, his eyes narrowing. 'You have me all figured out.'

'You're an easy read.'

What else could it be? Their marriage hadn't just been platonic, it had been positively frigid. Intellectually, they got along beautifully. They could talk business until the sun came up. But there had been no physical contact of any kind, not even when they had drunk more vodka together than was good for them. They would attend functions where couples were together in every sense of the word—holding hands, sneaking kisses. For all their cordiality, she and Nico wouldn't even wipe a fragment of lint from each other's clothing.

It was what she had signed up to. But she'd had no idea when she drew up that stupid contract that it would come to hurt so much and gnaw at her insides.

'If I were to tell you I find you incredibly sexy, would you think I was lying?'

'We both know I am not your type.' Even when passing her a mug of coffee he made a concerted effort not to touch her.

'Maybe my tastes are becoming more discerning.'

'Unluckily for you, *my* tastes aren't. If you think I want to share a bed with a man who has a deli counter of blondes queuing for a space in his bed, you have another think coming. Believe me, that was a strong positive for me when we made our no-sex pact.'

Nico studied her, his brow furrowed. 'Yet you were willing to share a bed with the ex-boyfriend you married me to escape?'

'There were numerous reasons I married you. Escaping Stephen was only one of them. Not having sex with you was another.'

He rose to his feet and flashed a smile. A dangerous smile. A predatory smile. 'Maybe if we had made sex part of our deal you would not be wanting to leave me. You certainly would not have needed to seek physical attention or *flowers* from your ex.'

Her incredulity at his arrogance was matched only by the heavy swirl of heat settling in her core.

Fighting it, she straightened to her full five foot three inches and speared him with a quelling look. 'Don't even go there. Don't even think about it. It's not going to happen. Not now. Not ever.'

'Ah, *daragaya*, but things have changed. You agreed to

give me a month to change your mind. And as we have never had sex before…' His words trailed off as he leaned over, and then he whispered into her ear. 'I guarantee one night with me and you will find your ex wanting. You will certainly never want to leave.'

It was the warmth of his breath in her ear, skewering her senses, that prevented her from slapping him. Tingles bounced on every millimetre of skin, her core thickening and nestling in the apex of her thighs, burning her.

'You're sick,' she dragged from her arid throat. 'You're like a child with an unwanted toy. You don't want to play with it, but the second another child picks it up you decide you want it after all. Well, I am not a toy. And I will not be treated as one.'

Nico had to admire her poise. Rosa walked away with her back straight and her hips gently swaying. She had not once raised her voice.

Yet that same fury she had displayed when she had told him of her wish to divorce was there, bubbling under the surface.

That passion, ripe for unleashing—how clearly he could see it now.

The logical part of his brain kept telling him to let her go, to give her the divorce she so obviously wanted and get on with his life.

He happened to believe that this time the logical part of his brain was wrong.

Maybe she was right in her 'child with a toy' analogy.

Her declaration a fortnight ago had released something within him—a fighting spirit more ruthless than in any business dealing he had ever conducted.

Nico hated to lose. He had spent the past fortnight ensuring he would win.

He and Rosa were bound by a piece of paper and two bands of gold. Nothing more. He had failed to appreciate that she was not an automaton. She was a sexual being, with needs and desires like everyone else. It was only natural she would seek gratification. On reflection, the only thing that should surprise him was how long it had taken her.

What he had *not* expected was the ugly, putrid feeling residing deep in his guts at the knowledge of what she had done.

He could not stop thinking about it.

She had gained satisfaction with another.

The thought of another man pawing *his wife* made his skin crawl.

The thought of his wife pawing another man made him want to punch a wall.

And now all bets were off.

Rosa's desire for a divorce meant whatever agreement they had made was null and void.

Soon she would share that delectable body with *him*. Her husband.

He hadn't intended to come on to her so soon, but the little stunt he had just pulled had proved one thing: he recognised the signs of feminine desire and in his strait-laced wife he had seen them. She wanted him. He would use that latent desire and play with her until she was begging for *his* possession, whimpering with the pleasure only *he* could give her, until all thoughts of another were eradicated from her mind.

He would make things so good she would never want to leave.

Rosa was buried nose-deep in paperwork when she heard the front door of the villa open. Every limb and digit froze.

She was determined every document would be faultless. There was nothing worse than thinking you had it word-perfect only for Nico to read through the documents and find a misspelled Russian word or an incorrect tense. Admittedly that had only happened twice, but that had been enough for her to determine it would not happen on this, their last trip together.

Not that she *should* be busting a gut for the man. Throughout their marriage he had treated her with nothing but professional courtesy. All right, maybe that was exaggerating things a little—whenever she had accompanied him to functions they had always had fun together, but it had been strictly platonic fun. Now it was all long, lingering glances and murmured comments that could be twisted into something intimate if she so chose.

She did not choose.

It would be obvious to a blind man what Nico was up to.

Soon he would make his move. And she would be ready for it.

A waft of citrusy musk wafted under her nose and she reached for her cup of cold coffee, washing away the saliva that had formed, Pavlov's Dog–style, in her mouth.

'How are you getting on?' To her intense irritation he placed one hand on her desk, the other on the back of her chair, and peered over her shoulder to see what she was working on.

'Fine, thank you.' She didn't dare move. He was so close his breath was tickling her hair, making her aware of the heat emanating from his powerful body. She could feel it now, that heat, and her whole body was alive and tingling at his proximity.

'Good. It is time to stop. We're going out for dinner.'

'Go without me. I've far too much work to do.' Actually, she didn't. She had been pleasantly surprised to find there was only a fraction of the expected workload, the reduction assisted by the half-dozen translators Nico had flown over to help her. At the rate she was ploughing through it she could be back in London within a week.

'Impossible. We are dining with Robert and his wife.'

'In that case I *definitely* have far too much work to do. And can you please move back and stop invading my personal space?'

His response to her request was to lean over her shoulder and flip the lid of her laptop shut.

Rosa's spine stiffened, then froze. She stared at the now closed laptop with widening eyes, her hands curling into fists as fury simmered through her veins. 'I've just spent three hours working on that document,' she said through gritted teeth.

'And now you have finished. Your working day is over.'

'I hadn't saved it.'

'Your laptop is configured to auto-save every five minutes. Any loss will be minimal.'

How *dared* he sound so reasonable? How dared he? '*I* decide when my working day is over. Not you.'

'Rosa, I do not recall giving you a choice in the matter. You are calling it a day and that is that. Now, go and get ready for dinner.'

Her frustrations spilling over, she deliberately shoved her chair back and 'accidentally' rammed it into Nico's legs. He jumped back.

'Sorry,' she lied, hastily getting to her feet.

He did not look in the least perturbed, simply threw her a lazy, knowing smile which she longed to slap off his face.

Keeping a good distance between them, she folded her arms across her chest and glared at him. 'You *do* realise Robert King thinks I'm here on a free jaunt? He probably thinks you've appointed me as your PA as some kind of tax dodge.'

She had absented herself from the meeting between Nico and Robert that morning in the hotel conference room with the excuse that she needed to ensure all the other translators had settled in. In reality she had left the conference room because if she had stayed another minute she would have been liable to throw her laptop at Robert King. It would not have been half as bad if Nico had not allowed Robert's misconceptions to continue.

'Why do you care what he thinks?' he asked. 'You're excellent at your job and he will realise it soon enough.'

'I don't like people making assumptions about me.'

Nico stored this little nugget of information away. It was extremely rare for Rosa to let slip anything personal about herself, however innocuous. He knew she was devoted to her job, knew her favourite food, knew she loved all things Russian, knew she could not sleep when travelling, knew she disliked raised voices and knew she was an orphan. Until now, that had been it.

Now he could add a dislike of people judging her to the list. Briefly he wondered where this dislike had come from, but pushed the thought away. It shouldn't—didn't—matter to him. It was the information itself he required.

Know your enemies. Know their weaknesses. The who, what, where, when and why were superfluous.

However, she did have a valid point about Robert's attitude towards her. Rosa was damn good at her job, and as smart as a whip, which was the main reason their marriage had been such a success—at least from his perspective. She was a good sounding board and able to see the bigger picture with the barest of facts. He had become accustomed to confiding in her about business, had almost come to rely on it.

His mouth filled with a bitter taste as he was reminded that, unless he changed her mind, one day some other man was going to get the benefit of that excellent brain.

He had done nothing to prevent Robert forming the wrong

opinion of her but he should feel no guilt. All was fair in love and war, and this was definitely war. He had taken a perverse pleasure in seeing her reduced to the status of wife and pretty trinket hanging on his arm.

His independent wife clung to her professional status like a second skin. She clung to her professional status around *him* like a second skin. She never let her guard down for a single second. Not even when she confessed infidelity. Always that wall was between them. He had facilitated its construction with her.

Well, he was going to tear it down—every last brick. By hook or by crook he would bring out that hidden womanly side, a side she had been happy to share with someone else.

Now he had got over his shock about her wanting to leave him he was able to think rationally. He could not in all conscience force her to stay if she was determined to go. It would be intolerable for them both. But neither was he prepared to let her go without sampling that fabulous body for himself and making her see how good things could be between them. Goddammit, she was his *wife*.

One thing he had learned about women was that one night in his bed was enough for them to start talking about *feelings*. Had he not married Rosa because she was nothing like those women?

Rosa was emotionally closed off. It was preposterous to imagine she would lie in bed and discuss *feelings,* or that she would expect him to share his.

His solution was perfect. The more he thought about it, the more it made sense. They would continue with their perfect marriage and in the evenings he would share her bed and her delectable body. That would stave off her loneliness and put paid to her ridiculous idea of divorce.

He smothered a sudden burst of mirth at the recognition

that at least he wouldn't have to worry about her hearing wedding bells.

'Rosa, I will make it clear to Robert tonight that you are more than just my wife, that you are an excellent translator and PA.'

'You most certainly will not,' she said, in what sounded uncannily like exasperation. 'That would be even worse.' She adopted a childish voice. *'Oh, Mr King, have I told you how well my little wife sings? She's so good she could be on a talent show.'*

Despite himself, Nico laughed. 'I get your point. I will try for subtlety. How does that sound?'

She narrowed her eyes. 'Better. Obviously it would have been better not to get us into this position in the first place. If you had just introduced me as your PA, like you always used to do, we would not have this problem.'

'I don't have any problem with it—I'm proud to call you my wife.'

Satisfaction drove through him as he witnessed the colour spread up her neck. He was only speaking the truth.

'But naturally I do understand why the situation would irk you.'

'Irk?' The caramel in her eyes darkened. 'Yes, I would say the situation *irks* me. I've worked too hard for my professionalism to be reduced to nothing but a bit part in your life.'

He could understand that too. And the guilt that had been hanging around him like a bad smell reeked a little bit stronger. Nico understood hard work. How else did a boy from a backward Siberian mining town break free and conquer the world?

'Is there something wrong with your neck?' he enquired.

'Sorry?'

'You keep kneading it. You were doing it this morning.'

'Oh.' For a moment she looked a little stunned. 'I cricked it last night.'

'Cricked?'

'I strained it. I woke up with it. I'll take some ibuprofen for it soon.'

'Is it from sleeping on the sofa?'

The look she gave him could only be described as a *'well, duh'* look.

He smiled. 'That is what happens when you allow pride to dictate your actions. There was a perfectly good bed for you to sleep in—there still is.'

'Or you could do the gentlemanly thing and offer to sleep on the sofa tonight.'

'I could,' he agreed. 'But I won't. The bed is plenty big enough for both of us. I promise I will not try anything with you.' He paused deliberately before continuing, 'That is not to say *you* cannot try anything with me.'

That delicious colour flared across her face and neck again. 'There you go again, making innuendoes and flirting with me.'

'That was not innuendo. It was fact. I would be delighted if you were to seduce me.'

Rosa looked as if she were about to bolt, so Nico raised his hands in a sign of peace. 'Robert and Laura are expecting to dine with us and it would be wholly embarrassing if I were to arrive solo.'

Deliberately he played to her sense of fairness—another trait he had forgotten to tuck away in his mental box of her characteristics.

From the pursing of her lips he could tell she was thinking about it. He pressed a little harder. 'All you have done since we left London is work. You need to take a break.'

'All right,' she relented grudgingly. 'I'll come with you. But I don't want a late night.'

'Not a problem. We have a busy day tomorrow, so an early night will do us both good.' Not that he would confide what type of busy day they would be sharing. If he were to tell her he was certain she would hijack a yacht and sail all the way to the mainland to catch a flight home.

'I'll go and get ready.' She slid past him and grabbed her handbag from the desk.

A tiny brown mole on the nape of her neck caught his attention. He had never noticed it before. Did she have others...?

A weird compulsion to press a kiss to it and taste that creamy skin crept through him. Before he could act on it she'd walked off, leaving him to blow out tiny puffs of air, struggling to control the ache spreading through his loins.

His physical reaction to a tiny mole perplexed him.

His growing physical reaction to *her* perplexed him.

All this flirting was becoming a major turn-on—which was strange in itself as he was not a man given to flirting. But Rosa's reaction to it was such an unexpected delighted that the more he did it, the more he wanted to do it.

Maybe he had been telling the truth when he'd said his tastes were becoming more discerning?

Women had always been an exotic mystery to him. He enjoyed sex, but he found intimacy on any other level repellent. He had certainly never before become fixated on a *mole*.

He was sure some psychoanalyst would put his repulsion down to being brought up solely by an undemonstrative father. Since leaving the Siberian mining town where he'd grown up, Nico had learned that some men displayed physical affection towards their children. Not his father. Mikhail Baranski was a real man's man: hard-drinking and hard-working. He had provided for Nico, but expected his son to take care of himself. All Nico's knowledge about physical affection and intimacy came from books. When he'd left home and moved to

Moscow he had assumed relationships would be as easy to conduct as they were in the books. But they weren't.

It had taken his relationship with Galina for him to realise he simply wasn't wired for it. Emotions and affection were for other people. Not for him. He had sampled failure once and had no intention of tasting it again.

His marriage to Rosa had been the perfect solution to this inbred aversion to intimacy. He had a discreet woman of intelligence to share his life, without any of the mumbo-jumbo sex seemed to provoke in the female of the species—the mumbo-jumbo that was totally alien to him.

CHAPTER FIVE

'WILL I DO?'

Nico looked up from his laptop and appraised his wife, who had just made an appearance from the bedroom.

She posed before him, hands on hips, chin cocked upwards. 'I assume the dress code is casual?'

She had finally released her ebony hair from the confines of that dreadful ponytail she favoured. She'd had it cut since the last time he had seen her wear it loose. Her silky locks still fell in waves down her back, but the front had been feathered, softening her angular features. Tonight she had opted for simplicity, wearing a demure dusky-pink dress that flared slightly to her knees and matching it with silver sandals with heels that added a good four inches to her short, curvy frame. Her concession to make-up was a touch of mascara and some pale pink lipstick. She looked wickedly pretty, but beneath the truculent expression he detected a hint of apprehension in her eyes.

He searched for the right words to tell her how beautiful she looked.

'You look fine,' he said. 'I'd better get ready. I've opened a bottle of white—it's in the fridge.'

He showered quickly and methodically, trying to banish the glimmer of hurt his off-hand compliment had briefly evoked in Rosa's eyes.

At first glance she was just a reasonably attractive woman. It wasn't until you studied her face and became trapped in the depth of those striking caramel eyes that you became aware of her radiant yet understated beauty. Unlike most other women, whose beauty faded after a couple of dates, becoming—dared he say it?—a touch boring, Rosa's beauty increased with each subsequent look. There was always something new to see: a new profile of her snub nose if looked at from a new angle, lines that appeared depending on whether she was smiling or frowning, lips that changed colour depending on her tiredness and mood.

By the time he had dressed, donning a short-sleeved navy linen shirt and charcoal chinos, and left the bedroom, Rosa was back at her desk. It didn't surprise him.

'What are you doing?'

She jumped and slammed down the lid of her laptop. 'Nothing.'

'Nothing? Really? Then why have your cheeks gone red?'

'It's personal.'

'Did you remember to save it before you closed the lid?' he asked pointedly.

Rosa's cheeks coloured even brighter. Her face tight, her lips clenched into a thin line, she got up from her chair and stalked past him, grabbing a small clutch bag off the table. 'Are we going?'

Nico briefly debated opening her laptop and doing a thorough investigation into what she had been up to.

'If we don't leave now we'll be late,' she reminded him. 'And we wouldn't want to be late for Robert and Laura, would we?'

What would his demanding answers achieve? He knew who she had been in touch with. If she hadn't been corresponding with Stephen why else would she be so evasive?

Swallowing the bile that had risen in his throat, and making a mental note to check out her laptop after she had fallen asleep, Nico locked the front door behind them and they set off.

'Why have you removed your shoes?' he asked, after glancing at her and realising she had shrunk. The top of her head was once again barely level with his armpit.

'Believe me, these shoes are not made for walking.'

'So why wear them?'

'I'm not. I'm carrying them.'

'Your feet will get cut.'

'This pathway's so smooth I bet Robert's had the sweepers out.'

There was not a lot he could say to that type of logic—especially when his mind was still consumed with rabid, ugly thoughts.

He had to know.

'Have you heard from him?'

'Who?'

'Stephen.'

Her answer came succinctly. 'No.'

'Do you think you will hear from him again?'

A mirthless sound that might have been some form of laugh escaped from her throat. 'Nico, it was a disaster. I should never have gone out with him...' Her voice trailed off before she added quietly, 'I doubt Stephen will ever want to see me again.'

But did she want to see *him* again? For some reason the question stuck in his throat.

And if she hadn't been corresponding with Stephen then what *had* she been up to on the laptop?

'How did you meet up with him again?' he asked, keeping his voice on a nice, even keel. 'I thought you had cut him out of your life?'

'I had.'

Deliberately he let the silence envelop them.

'I bumped into him a couple of months ago at the dealership when I went to buy my new car.'

'You have a new car?'

'Yes.'

'What did you get?'

'A Fiat 500.'

'Ah, yes. I recall seeing it in the garage. I assumed it was Gloria's. Why didn't you go for something more selective?'

'By "selective" I assume you mean more expensive?'

'*Da.* If it was a matter of cost, I would have been happy to pay for it.'

'That's very generous, Nico, but I've made it perfectly clear I don't want your money.'

'You are my wife, Rosa. I appreciate ours is not a conventional marriage but it still means something. If you need anything you only have to ask.' In eleven months of marriage she hadn't asked for anything from him. She really was—had been—the perfect wife.

They arrived at the hotel, pausing for a moment so Rosa could put her shoes back on before walking into the lobby. He felt her stiffen beside him and knew without asking that she had seen Laura King, who was propped against the bar, towering over her diminutive husband.

At the functions they'd attended as a married couple he had noticed the way Rosa's generous smile would not quite meet her eyes when she was introduced to the starlets and models that littered the social scene. Often he had wondered if she disapproved of them—an irrelevant question he had never before felt compelled to ask.

She'd displayed the same stiffness then as she was displaying now, with Laura looming towards her.

It suddenly dawned on him that it was not disapproval she felt. He didn't know what it could be—and neither should he care—but in that brief moment of understanding a strange compulsion swept through him, an impulse to wrap his arm around her and offer reassurances that everything would be fine.

Internally he recoiled. The idea of offering comfort, or re-assurance, or *anything* of a physical nature beyond sex, was anathema to him. He didn't have a clue what the require-ments of such an act were, and nor would he know the right words to say.

His rare bout of indecision was steamrollered over by Rob-ert swooping on Rosa and pulling her into an exuberant em-brace.

'You look beautiful, Mrs Baranski.' He beamed, letting her go but taking her hand and planting a kiss on it.

Robert King was easily in his seventies, and Butterfly Is-land was but a small part of his empire. King Island, an un-inhabited island he also owned, was to be used as a base for Nico's miners. If the contracts were not signed Nico could forget about mining offshore.

At that precise moment, though, Nico wanted nothing more than to pull the old man away from his wife and tell him to keep his liver-spotted hands to himself.

But of course he did nothing of the sort, and nor did he understand where this primitive, possessive urge had come from. He could only assume the heat of the day had some-how got to him.

Robert made the introductions and then led them through to the restaurant, which was as lush and opulent as the rest of the resort.

Rosa could not help but wish they were dining outside, in one of the beachside restaurants, where the soft breeze would cool them naturally, rather than inside with the air-conditioning turned on full-blast. She shivered and rubbed her arms, wishing she could move a little closer to Nico and take advantage of his body heat.

Robert looked at Nico. 'Red or white?'

'Do you have Pouilly-Fumé on your wine list?' Nico asked

'We certainly do.' Robert clicked his fingers and a waiter, who had been hovering on the sidelines, practically flew over.

'Do you want white too, Rosa?' Nico asked pointedly.

Rosa suppressed a smile.

Now that she was seated, and had got over her shock at seeing Robert's wife, she had started to relax a little.

Somewhere in her imaginings she had conjured up an image of an elderly, yet perfectly coiffured and immaculately dressed lady—a kind of glamorous gran. The reality was markedly different. Laura King, who wasted no time in bragging that she had once worked as a model, was a good forty years her husband's junior, and stood a good foot taller than him too. She was stunning: ultra-tanned and toned, with long sun-bleached blonde hair that fell in a sheet to a pert derrière enhanced by a tiny gold dress.

In short, she was everything Rosa wasn't.

From feeling happy with the outfit she had selected, Rosa now felt utterly flat. She could not help but imagine Nico comparing the two women—his rather plain wife seated next to him opposed to the glittery beauty opposite.

Nico wouldn't have to pretend with Laura. He would want to make love to her for herself, and not out of ferocious pride. The same pride that would not allow anyone to know he had shared a roof with a woman for almost a year without once becoming intimate with her.

He would never have stood *Laura* up on her birthday.

It made her belly curdle and her blood simmer to know he only thought of her, Rosa, as an asset in his successful life. He wanted to keep this asset, neatly ticked off in the box marked 'wife', not because he didn't want to lose *her,* per se, but because he didn't want to lose. Full stop.

He would never want her for herself.

Whatever she wore, however much money she spent, Rosa would never be anything but a distant star compared with Laura's dazzling sun. Judging from the less than subtle glances being thrown her way, she had a feeling the Amazonian agreed.

'How long have you two been married?' Laura asked in a syrupy voice.

'Eleven months.'

'Eleven and a half months,' Nico corrected.

'Oh, so you're still newlyweds! And what are you planning for your first anniversary? Something special?'

'Oh, yes,' Rosa agreed sweetly. No way would she allow her feelings of intimidation to show. 'I'm planning to divorce him.' She cast a quick glance at Nico, to see how he had taken her off-the-cuff quip. His face was set in its usual impassive mask.

Laura squealed with laughter. 'That is so *funny.*'

'Isn't it? How long have you two been married?'

Laura fluttered her extended lashes at her husband. 'Three years. It feels like for ever—doesn't it, darling?'

The conversation went rapidly downhill. Laura completely dominated it, mostly throwing sugar-laced barbs at her husband and casting lingering eyes at Nico when she thought no one was looking. For his part, Robert seemed oblivious to his wife's behaviour, beaming throughout.

After the main course Laura excused herself to 'powder her nose', while Robert insisted there were new guests he needed to welcome.

'Are you all right?' Nico asked quietly once they were alone.

'Me? I'm fine.'

'She is a little…full-on.'

'Who? Laura? I can't say I noticed,' she lied, compressing her lips together.

'She is certainly a handful.'

Rosa fixed a thin smile to her face. It was the most she could manage.

'It seems to me Robert has his work cut out keeping her in line.'

'I doubt anyone could keep *her* in line,' she retorted tartly. Did Nico *have* to talk about that woman? 'Besides, they're made for each other.'

Nico raised a brow.

'He gets a beautiful young bimbo on his arm; she gets to inherit billions when he dies.'

'I've never known you to be such a cynic,' he mused.

She took a long sip of wine and then quickly put the glass back down. Her tongue was starting to loosen—a sure sign it was time to switch to water.

There was something else eating away at her too: a low, queasy ache that clutched at her chest and swirled in her belly, making her want to pounce on the Amazonian and tell her to keep her manicured mitts off her husband.

But Nico was not going to be her husband for much longer. In any event, she had no proprietorial rights to him. Theirs was an open marriage. There were no propriety rights. Even if he was trying to establish some for his own ends.

'So you think she is beautiful?' Nico asked, his voice mild, uninterested.

'Of course. Don't you?' She almost laughed. As if Nico would think Laura anything *but* a beautiful sun. Physically, she was exactly his type. No wonder he couldn't stop talking about her—and this from a man who never talked anything but business.

After a pause, Nico said, 'Anyone who spends that amount

of time, money and effort on herself could not look anything but beautiful.'

Flattened, Rosa nearly reached for her wine again, but then she froze, suddenly aware of Nico leaning over into her personal space. He put his mouth to her ear, close enough for her to feel the warmth of his breath.

All at once her heart-rate tripled.

Tingles of awareness spread throughout her skin, like hot treacle swimming under the surface, throbbing down low, deep in her core.

Her mouth ran dry as this one intimate moment consumed her entire being.

Whatever Nico had planned to whisper was cut off as Robert came back to the table, breaking the spell with an almost tangible snap.

'Excuse me, lovebirds,' he said, winking at them as he took his seat. 'Sorry to interrupt.'

'You are not interrupting anything,' Nico said with his usual calmness, draping a casual arm across Rosa's back.

Laura chose that moment to make a reappearance too. From the manic way she was speaking, and the amount of sniffing she was now doing, Rosa suspected she had taken the term 'powder her nose' literally.

There were not many people she disliked, but Laura King was fast becoming one of them. Generally she tried not to judge a book by its cover—even beautiful, leggy women— but if that woman fluttered her eyelashes at Nico one more time she swore she would stick a fork in her leg.

As consolation, she reminded herself that they only had around a week left on this island, and then she would never have to see Laura again.

She wouldn't have to see Nico again either.

She took her glass and finished the wine in one swallow.

'Is something the matter?' Nico asked.

She shivered. 'Someone walked over my grave.'

It was almost the truth. For that brief moment the thought of leaving him had felt like a bereavement.

She had to remind herself she was doing the right thing.

Marrying Nico had triggered something inside her. At first it had been so subtle she hadn't noticed it, but as time had gone on it had crept under her skin and into her psyche. No matter how hard she'd tried to keep her distance, no matter how hard she'd tried to keep their relationship professional and companionable, that something had fought to be heard.

She had run from it. She had refused to work permanently for him because of it, blithely covering her ears in a futile attempt to drown out the noise and pretend it didn't exist.

Well, she heard it loud and clear now.

Desire. Lust. Need. Whatever name you gave it, it amounted to the same thing.

She didn't want to need anyone—least of all Nico.

The sooner they completed this project the better.

Leaving Nico had never felt so imperative.

'You're looking peaky, lady.' Robert's booming voice broke through her red-coloured thoughts.

Nico's turned his head, his sharp eyes narrowing as he studied her. 'Another ghost?' he asked ironically.

'I think now would be a good time to let her in on the surprise you have arranged,' Robert said.

A sudden sense of dread washed over her. Whatever Nico had been plotting, it could not be good news.

His arrogant grin confirmed this opinion before he even opened his mouth. 'Robert has kindly agreed to let us take a little trip on one of his yachts. Just the two of us. It's my anniversary present for you.'

Rosa was glad Nico had declined Robert's offer of a golf-buggy to drive them back to their villa. She needed fresh air to think, and this clear, warm night with a delicious breeze from the ocean was the perfect setting to do just that. Well, it would be if she was alone, not walking by the side of the man who had put her in such a pickle.

'Are you not going to remove your shoes?'

'Sorry?'

'Your crippling shoes.' Nico stopped and nodded at her feet.

'Right. Yes. You're right.' Her head was full of so much confusion she had completely forgotten her feet were killing her. Of course now he had mentioned it she felt the full force of her shoes' constriction and quickly took them off. But not before debating stamping on his foot first.

Why did he have to display proper concern at the moment when she wanted nothing more than to bodily harm him?

'When are you going to start scolding me?' he asked, with a definite hint of anticipation.

'What's the point?' She shrugged tightly. 'You're clearly one step ahead of me.'

When Nico had made his announcement he had placed his hand on her thigh and squeezed it gently. To the casual observer it would have been a sign of affection. To Rosa it had been a warning.

He had been counting on her not making a scene and, god-damn him, he had counted correctly.

She would sooner cut her thumbs off than have a scene in public—or a scene anywhere, for that matter.

And so she had smiled sweetly and thanked Nico and Robert for the lovely, thoughtful gesture. At the same time she had placed her own hand on Nico's thigh. She had tried hard not to notice the muscular strength as she dug her nails in as hard as she could and said, 'You conniving bastard,' in Russian.

He had translated this to the rapt Kings as, 'You are a wonderful husband.' At least Robert had looked rapt. Rosa's one small consolation was that Laura's immovable face had looked positively sulky.

How she had longed to lash out at him properly—still longed to. How dared he manipulate her in such a fashion?

The fury racing through her was only matched by the tendrils of excitement unfurling in her stomach—tendrils she wanted to find scissors for and snip dead.

All these emotions were terrifying. The only way she could cope was to suck it up and ride it out. In no way, shape or form would she allow Nico to glean how deeply he'd affected her.

Was this how hormonal teenagers felt? Rosa had never been a proper hormonal teenager. Not for her the lashing out or falling off the rails that befell so many other adolescents. Who had there been for her to lash out at? The one person she had really wanted to kick out at, namely her mother, hadn't been there. Her mother had gone. No forwarding address. No Rosa.

Now the additional translators made sense. Nico could whisk her off for the day without affecting the contract schedule and everyone would think how romantic he was.

This one gesture more than any other killed the annulment idea stone-dead.

She would suck it up. It was only for one day. She could cope with Nico for one day.

'Did you bring a bikini?'

'No.' And if she had she wouldn't wear it in front of him.

'Why not?'

'We are supposed to be here to work, not go day-tripping on a yacht.'

'We are in one of the most beautiful locations in the world. Surely you brought some clothes to relax in?'

With the exception of a couple of dresses, the clothes she had brought were decidedly practical. She mentally ran through her wardrobe, trying to think of something suitable she could wear for a day's cruising.

'Never mind,' he said, interrupting her private musings. 'I'll arrange for a member of staff to bring a bikini for you from the resort boutique.'

'Can you make sure it's a *burkhini*?' she could not resist saying. She would bet Nico had never seen cellulite. At least not in the flesh.

'What is that?'

'Never mind.' She sighed. 'Go ahead. Do what you like. You generally do.'

'You're learning.'

They had arrived back at the villa. Nico dug his hand into his pocket for the key.

'Is your neck still hurting?' he asked as he unlocked the door, holding it open for her.

'Yes. And, no, I don't want a massage, thank you.' Her throat caught and she turned her face away. It shouldn't have surprised her that he had noticed something wrong with her neck—Nico noticed *everything*. Yet it had. His simple concern had touched her in a way she could hardly bear to think about.

'I do not recall offering one,' he said smoothly. 'However, I *am* prepared to do the gentlemanly thing and let you have the bed tonight.'

'Where will you sleep?'

'I will take the sofa.'

She stared at him, wondering what was going on in that conniving mind. He looked back at her with an openness she found suspicious, certain it was not simple concern dictating his offer.

'Why would you do that?'

He reached out and stroked a finger under one of her eyes. 'Believe it or not, *daragaya*, I am not a complete bastard. You have been working hard and need to rest.'

* * *

Nico felt her quiver, then stiffen beneath his touch, and experienced a frisson of satisfaction.

How easy it would be to kiss those plump, delectable lips. Rosa would certainly explode—although whether it would be an explosion of lust or an explosion of all the unleashed anger she was trying so hard to contain he could not say.

There would be plenty of time on the yacht for seduction. When it happened, he wanted her to be fully committed to it. He wanted Rosa begging for him.

He did not want her looking at him with eyes bruised from lack of sleep...eyes that no longer looked at him with total trust. Whenever she looked at him now it was with suspicion.

When she had looked at her ex, what had been ringing out of those caramel eyes? Had it been adoration?

She'd said sleeping with Stephen had been a disaster. The thought brought him no comfort. She had allowed another man to make love to her. He could not rid himself of the nasty taste that left in his mouth.

As cruel as he knew it was to think such thoughts, he hoped Stephen was an impotent flop.

When he, Nico, made love to Rosa, it would be the most satisfying, fulfilling event of her life.

But now was not the time to make his move. Rosa no longer trusted him. She was right not to. He needed to regain that trust.

But first he needed to check her laptop, and the easiest way to do that would be by letting her sleep in the bedroom with the door closed.

He dropped his hand and ran it through his hair. 'Go to bed, Rosa,' he said, 'Before I change my mind and join you.'

His lips twitched as she pointed her nose in the air and walked off, swinging her sandals.

An hour later, he threw the sheet back and swung his legs

off the sofa. Silently he padded to the office of the villa, pausing as he passed the bedroom. A dim glow seeped under the closed door. Rosa was still awake.

He filled his lungs with oxygen, debating whether to climb back into his makeshift bed and get some sleep.

Impossible. Until he knew what she had been doing his brain would not switch off. She had been up to something. That was a given. She had reacted like a startled rabbit and he wanted to know why. He *needed* to know why.

His antennae were on high alert. If he were a dog he would have an ear cocked. He flipped the lid of her laptop and turned it on. He flinched as the brief start-up tune rang out.

Keeping still, hardly daring to breathe, he waited for movement from the bedroom. Nothing.

The laptop finished loading. Adrenaline firing through his veins, his heart pounding, he clicked the mouse.

It was password-protected.

He muttered an oath under his breath and racked his brains, trying to think of what she would use. As much as it sickened him even to key in the letters, the first word he tried was *Stephen*. Invalid. A warning came up that he had two further attempts before the laptop shut itself down. At that moment he heard the distant sound of the toilet in the *en suite* bathroom flushing.

A cold sweat enveloped him.

What the *hell* was he playing at?

He was trying to hack into his own wife's laptop. What kind of sick puppy was he?

Clicking on the 'shutdown' icon, he closed the lid and moved stealthily back to the sofa.

All was quiet in the villa. All except the thunder that was his heart.

CHAPTER SIX

AFTER A LIGHT breakfast they made their way via golf-buggy to the harbour. Awaiting them, gleaming brightly in the calm ocean, stood the *Butterfly King*, a majestic yacht eighty feet long and three decks high.

'Is it to your liking?' Nico asked, unable to gauge Rosa's reaction to it because her lips had formed such a tight white line.

'It is nice and big—so, yes, I would say it is perfect.'

'Well, that's good to know,' he murmured, 'that you find big things perfect.' He laughed softly at the filthy look she threw at him. 'Shall we board?'

He really was going to have to put a stop to all these innuendoes, he thought ruefully a few minutes, later when the ache in his loins still refused to abate.

If he'd known how much fun it would be to flirt with his strait-laced wife he would have tried it months ago. She coloured so beautifully.

But then, their marriage had never been about flirting. Their marriage had been strictly business.

Now their marriage was open season—nothing was off-limits.

The Captain led them through to a plush saloon, where he introduced them to the four other crew members. 'I'll leave Jim here to show you around,' he said. 'It's time to set sail.'

'Can I order you any refreshments before I give you the grand tour?' Jim asked.

'I think we could both do with a coffee,' Nico said quickly. He wanted to make sure they were far from shore before he sprang his next surprise.

'I'd love a cappuccino, thank you,' said Rosa. She walked over to the wide window and gazed out, giving him an excellent view of her rear.

His wife had proper womanly curves. The cream linen trousers she wore accentuated the shape of her rounded bottom, and the pale pink blouse displayed her tiny waist. Not for the first time he marvelled that he had been so blind to it.

After they had finished their coffee, and he judged they had sailed far enough that she would not attempt to swim back to shore, he announced it was time for the tour.

'I thought Jim was going to do it,' she said.

'There is no need to disturb him. I am well acquainted with the yacht's interior.' He threw out his arms expansively. 'As you can see, this is the saloon. Through that door is the dining room, which leads on to the gym. The lower deck is of no relevance to us, but the upper deck...' He smiled.

Rosa did not trust that smile. And nor did she trust the gleam in his eyes. 'The upper deck, what?'

'Come. I will show you.'

As soon as they set foot inside the door at the top of the stairs she knew she had been right to be suspicious.

'Is this some kind of joke?'

The entire top deck was a suite. Not just any suite, either. This was a suite designed for lovers.

The bed, all scarlet silk sheets and soft, plump pillows, easily took up a third of the space. It did not so much dominate. The bed *was* the space. A whole cabal of honeymooners could sleep on it. Everything was designed around it.

Bed! Sex!

She might as well scream the words out because this suite was designed with nothing but sex in mind. Even the swimming pool—yes it had a heart-shaped swimming pool at one end through some patio doors—was an extension of the romantic and yet somehow erotic theme. Whoever had designed this suite should either be commended for an award or shot.

'Nice try,' she said, backing away. '*You* can spend the day in this boudoir. Me? I'm going to sit in the saloon and drink lots of vodka.'

'Look in the dressing room,' he instructed, pointing at a door.

She'd bet he'd had a minuscule bikini put there for her.

She was right. What she had not anticipated was the amount of other clothing neatly hung in there too.

Spinning round to face him, she put her hands on her hips. 'How long are we staying here?'

'A week.'

There was no other word for it. 'Bastard.'

When she would have walked out, there and then, he grabbed her wrist and pulled her to him. 'Come outside with me for a minute.'

'No. I'm going to see the Captain and demand he return us to shore.' She tried to shake him off but his grip was too strong.

'It will not make any difference.'

'Why? Have you paid him off?'

He didn't even have the decency to look shamefaced.

'You bloody well have, haven't you?'

Nico released his grip and tugged at her hand. He led her outside, past the swimming pool to the front of the yacht. She was so steaming mad she let him.

'Look at this scenery,' he said once they were standing side-by-side, holding on to the railings. 'Look at the calm of the ocean. You need a holiday. I need a holiday. Neither of us has taken any time off for over a year.'

She had to admit there was something rather soothing about the glistening ocean. 'Yes, I need a holiday. One far, far away from *you*. I can't believe you would do something so...so...' She scrambled around in her fried brain for the correct word. 'So sneaky.'

'I had to be sneaky because I knew you wouldn't agree to it otherwise.'

'Too right I wouldn't have.'

'Forgive me for being underhand. I am trying to save our marriage. Desperate times call for desperate deeds.' He gave her a crooked smile and lightly covered her hand with his. His wedding ring glistened under the beaming sun. 'You said you would give me a month, but it seems to me you have already made up your mind that our marriage is over.'

'Other than flirting with me, you haven't done anything to convince me otherwise.'

'I appreciate I was busy for the first two weeks, but a lot of that time was spent organising this.'

'Really?' She experienced a flicker of uncertainty.

'Really. I needed to ensure a good team of staff were left at the resort so you and I could take this week off and get to know each other properly.' Nico's features had a seriousness to them that had been missing in recent days. 'It seems to me that you are being unfair.'

'How have you worked that out?'

'You came to Butterfly Island with your mind made up. You promised to give me—us—another chance, but you didn't mean it, did you?'

'What's the point?' she said with a shrug, turning her focus back onto the open water. 'You only want our marriage to continue for your own convenience and ego.'

'My point exactly. You came here with preconceived ideas

about what I want and what my motives are and have not given two thoughts to the fact I genuinely want our marriage to work. For both of us.'

His low yet gentle tones made her squirm inside, like a naughty schoolgirl caught stuffing crayons in her pockets.

'How do you imagine that makes me feel?' he continued. 'Knowing you are only pretending? That in reality you are counting the days until you can be rid of me?'

This time she squirmed visibly. When he put it like that it did seem rather cold. She hadn't meant it to be. It was self-preservation. Nothing else.

'Give me this week, Rosa. Let us get to know each other properly—the way we should have done from the start.'

She wanted to. She didn't know where it came from, but she felt her chest expand, as if it were full of fluttering butterflies trying desperately to break free.

She had got by perfectly well on her own. In all the years she had been with Stephen she had always felt detached from him and that was the way she liked it. With Nico she could feel her detachment slipping. And it terrified her.

'But all this,' she said, turning around and waving an arm towards the suite. 'This doesn't feel like the action of a man trying to get to know me better. This feels like the action of a man trying to get into my knickers.'

How could she trust that he wanted *her* knickers off? *Her. Rosa.* Not his *wife.* Not his *asset.* Her. A woman he desired.

'Can it not be both?' His green eyes held hers, burning her with their intensity. 'I am not going to deny that I desire you. But I am prepared to wait until you are ready. You know you can trust me.'

'We always said no sex,' she said.

Cornered did not begin to describe how hemmed in she felt at that moment. She had trusted Nico enough to marry him, but that had not required any intimacy—nothing physical or emotional. Their marriage had given her the things she truly craved—stability and a feeling of belonging, of being a unit. Just sharing the same surname had been enough. At least it had been. For the first few months.

How could she trust that he wouldn't reject her like everyone else she had loved in her life? She couldn't. She didn't know how.

'That rule did neither of us any good, did it? The loneliness of an empty bed drove you into the arms of your ex. If our marriage is to continue, there is no doubt in my mind that sex needs to be a part of it. We need to have a proper marriage.'

Nico could see Rosa fighting a war with herself. Victory was within his grasp. He could smell it. He should have played to her sense of fairness from the start. After all, it was the thing he admired about her for above everything else.

That night in California, when the mad idea to marry had overtaken them and she had produced that piece of paper for them to write their contract, she could have made any number of demands on his fortune. But that was not Rosa's style. The first thing she had written was that neither would have a claim on the other's wealth. When he had queried this she had given that husky laugh and said, 'I don't want you thinking you can have a share of my flat. I earned it. You can keep all your billions. You earned them. I just want to keep my flat.'

She had been serious. For all the vodka they had consumed, he had known she was serious. Call him a fool—his lawyer, when they'd returned to England with the marriage certificate, certainly had—but he had trusted her.

Goddammit it, he had *trusted* her. Nico, the man who did not trust anyone, had trusted his wife. And she had slept with her ex.

The second point on the list had been no sex between them. The third point had been to allow either of them to take lovers so long as they exercised discretion. He had never dreamed Rosa would be the one to take advantage of that point.

Had she laughed with Stephen? Had he been the recipient of that throaty huskiness?

When had he, Nico, last heard that laugh?

He forced his mind back to the subject at hand. He had no intention of Rosa ever discovering how his veins burned with fury whenever he thought of them together.

'Give me this week. If at the end of it you still want to leave then I will not try to stop you. All I ask is that you keep an open mind. We can be good together. All you need to do is give us a chance to find out how good.'

He didn't realise he was holding his breath until, after long, interminable seconds, she finally inclined her head.

'It's obvious I'm stuck here, whether I like it or not. I'm not going to lie and pretend I'm thrilled at the way you have manipulated me. But I do get where you're coming from.' She turned her head and fixed her beautiful yet still wary eyes on him. 'I'm not going to make any promises other than I will *try* to keep an open mind about us.'

'I can't ask for any more than that.' He raised a hand and trailed the back of a finger down her cheek. She really had the most marvellous skin. 'Why don't you get changed into something with more of a holiday feel and I'll get us some drinks? We can sit out here, laze by the pool…the choice is yours.'

Her brow furrowed. 'The choice of what?'

'The choice to do what people on holiday do.'

'But I've never been on holiday before.'

'Seriously?'

A part of him thought she must be joking, while another part pointed out that neither of them had taken a break in the fifteen months they had known each other. They hadn't even bothered pretending to take a honeymoon. She had taken her holiday entitlement from her new job to accompany him as his assistant now, not expecting to be given the opportunity to let her hair down.

When, he wondered, did his wife ever let her hair down?

Had she let her hair down with Stephen?

'You can hardly talk,' she pointed out. 'When did *you* last take a holiday?'

That made him think. 'It must have been around eighteen months ago.' Before Rosa had come to work for him. 'But as a rule I like to take a week off every six months to recharge my batteries. In future it's something we can do together.'

Nico never holidayed with women. His relationships, if they could be called that, never lasted long enough. Once, he and Galina had discussed travelling together, or rather Galina had angled for it...

He swallowed and scratched the thought away. Travelling with Galina would have been a nightmare. She would have suffocated him.

He preferred going away with Serge and the rest of his old buddies from university, whether it was mountain climbing or trekking through the Amazon. Rosa was the only woman he would ever consider holidaying with. He doubted she could ever irritate him. She would certainly never try to suffocate him.

She gave a non-committal shrug. 'We'll see. I don't think I'm a holiday-type person.'

'What does that mean?'

'Holidays are things other people have. Not people like me.'

There was something in her voice, an almost confused ring, that pulled at him. It occurred to him that apart from reading the occasional book or watching the occasional film she rarely relaxed in the traditional sense.

Why had he never noticed that before?

'Everyone deserves a holiday,' he told her. 'Now, go and get changed and I'll meet you back out here shortly.'

Who had Nico shared his last holiday with? Rosa wondered, stepping into the dressing room and rifling through the items in there, all of which were marked with the name of a boutique from the King resort. She marvelled that they were the correct size, until she considered that *someone*—namely Nico—must have gone through her wardrobe. When had he done that? Back in London? At the villa? He had gone to huge trouble to make this happen, especially as the contract negotiations with Robert King were at such a delicate point.

She could not shake the feeling that she was being manipulated. Scratch that. *Of course* she was being manipulated— and blatantly so. He was not trying to hide it or make any excuses for it. Nico wanted their marriage to continue and was using all the means at his disposal to make it happen.

Was it possible his motives were sincere?

Was it truly possible he liked her enough as a person and desired her enough as a woman to fight to keep her in his life?

She could not wrap her head around it. Other than Stephen, people had generally fought to keep her *out* of their lives, not in it.

Deep in her belly was the sense that something was amiss. Try as she might to think of what it might be, she could not.

Maybe it would be best if she stopped thinking so much.

Settling on a black bikini, which she covered with a pair of denim shorts and a dusky-pink T-shirt, she smothered her exposed flesh with sunscreen and headed to the sundeck, studiously avoiding looking at the bed.

She had a whole day of Nico's sole company to get through before she could even contemplate sharing a bed with him— not just tonight but every night for the rest of the week. For once there would be nothing to distract her. No work. Nothing to keep her mind occupied from him.

He filled her mind too much as it was.

Rosa took a seat at an the outdoor table where a stack of boxes had been placed. Already bored with her own company, she took a look at them.

A moment later she almost choked when Nico strode up the stairs from the second deck to join her, carrying a couple of tall glasses. Not only had he removed his ever-present suit, but he had changed into a pair of knee-length canvas shorts. And nothing else. Nothing but hot, rippling muscle.

All of a sudden the heat of the day sank into her pores, making her feel clammy and bothered.

'You look hot,' he observed, taking a seat and pushing a glass towards her. 'This will cool you down.'

'What is it?'

'A cocktail.'

She sniffed the green concoction suspiciously. It smelled fresh and delicious. Taking a sip, she felt her eyes nearly pop out of her head. 'Blimey—this is strong. What's in it?'

He bestowed upon her an enigmatic smile. 'Enjoy it and leave the ingredients to me.'

'I never had you pegged as a cocktail fan.'

'When I was at university my dorm-mate threw a cocktail party. His cocktails were so disgusting I took over the bar.'

'I think you're yummy.'

She winced at the unintentional *faux pas*. But, seriously, how was she supposed to think straight with Nico's golden torso right in her line of vision? On the occasions when she had seen him in shorts and T-shirt for his daily jog she had been able to tune his incredible body out. That ability had now deserted her. But then, she had never seen him topless before—had never seen for herself the breadth of his shoul-

ders or the dusting of silky black hair covering his muscular chest that continued down to the low-slung shorts resting
on his hips.

'Sorry, I think *this*—the cocktail—is yummy.'

'Rosa, relax.' Nico's hand hovered in the air and for one
breathless moment she thought he was going to touch her.

Relax? *Relax?* How could she relax when just being near
him put her on hyper-alert?

'I'm not going to jump on you,' he murmured with a lazy
curve of his lips. 'Not until you ask me to or, even better,
jump on me.'

'You'll have a long wait,' she said. Even to her own ears
her voice sounded feeble. If only he would cover his chest
she would be able to think clearly.

His eyes darkened and gleamed. 'You will find I have incredible patience when it comes to something I really want.'

Rosa grabbed her cocktail and took a long sip, welcoming
the cold liquid's cooling effect on her flushing cheeks. 'Pack it
in, Nico. I've already told you I'm not making any promises.'

'I was merely making an observation,' he said smoothly,
placing a hand on the boxes. 'What would you like to play?
We have chess, Scrabble and backgammon. Or...' he wiggled
an eyebrow '...we could play something else entirely.'

Despite herself she snickered. She had to admit there was
something compelling about this irreverent, flirty Nico. She
wondered if this was how he treated his lovers and immediately scratched the thought away.

'I'll play you at a board game but you'll have to choose
which. I've never played any of them.'

He gave her the same look he'd given her when she told
him she'd never had a holiday.

'That's no problem. I'll go back to the saloon and select
some different games.'

'Don't worry about it,' she said. 'I doubt I'll know those

either. Why don't you teach me Scrabble? I've always wanted to learn that.'

It didn't take long for him to set the board up and go through the rules with her.

'Are you sure you've never played before?' he asked half an hour later. He had beaten her only by the skin of his teeth.

'Never,' she confirmed.

'Hmm.' He fixed disbelieving eyes on her. 'I think I'm in the hands of a Scrabble shark.'

Food was brought up for their lunch—a platter of refreshing fruits and cheeses. After they had demolished the lot Nico, unwilling to relinquish his bartending duties to anyone, made a pitcher of what he called 'a vodka cocktail', which had striped red and orange colours running through it.

Rosa won the second game. Fortified by more colourful cocktails than was good for her, she could not stop laughing about it—especially when Nico pretended to sulk.

'Ha!' she snorted. 'Beaten by a girl.'

'That's a very sexist remark, young lady,' he said, adopting a mock-grave voice.

She swept the tiles into the small green sack and flashed him a saccharine smile. 'That's because you're a very sexist man.'

His brows shot up. 'In what possible way am I sexist? I employ hundreds of women, many of them at senior or director level. I would employ more if the mining industry was not so male-dominated. We don't get enough women applying for positions.'

'That would be a valid point, but I don't think you see the women you employ as female.'

'You are confusing me.'

'It seems to me that if a woman isn't a tall, blonde stick-insect with silicone boobs you don't recognise her as a woman. She's just another drone in your employ.'

'If I were to flirt with any woman in my employ I would be asking for trouble. It's a sexual harassment lawsuit waiting to happen.'

'Possibly,' she conceded. 'Or it could just be that you don't fancy a woman who has to use her brains to earn a living rather than her body.'

'Ouch.' He winced. 'How does that theory explain why I fancy you?'

'It doesn't—but that's because you *don't* fancy me. Not really. You just don't like losing, and for me to leave our marriage means you'll have lost.'

CHAPTER SEVEN

For a moment it felt as if Rosa had looked inside his head and scoffed at what she found.

'Which brings me to the second point of my argument,' she continued, her husky voice full of amusement. 'You married a drone instead of a stick-insect because you assumed marrying a high-maintenance supermodel would be hell on earth. Did you ever seriously consider marrying any of your lovers?'

Fascinated, Nico shook his head.

Rosa was pretty much bang on the money.

Growing up, he had had minimal contact with the opposite sex. For twenty-one years women had been a remote, alien species.

And then he had met Galina, the first woman to prove to him that females were not a mysterious sub-gender.

Beautiful, intelligent, emotionally needy Galina...

Whenever he thought about her he could still taste failure on his tongue. Thinking about her always served as a reminder of why it was for the best for him to divide the women in his life into two camps.

In the first camp were his lovers—beautiful socialites who looked good on his arm. He was not so immodest as not to know he was fortunate in his looks and physique, but when it came to socialites those particular attributes came a low second to the size of his wallet. He was certain he could look like the Hunchback of Notre Dame and they would still want him. The thought of marrying any of them filled him with horror. As sexy and as beautiful as they were, the thought of waking up to one of them, sharing a roof, the demands they would place on him, were all things he found intolerable.

In the second camp were the women who worked for him, women employed for their brains and not their looks. As he had found with Galina, intelligent women tended to be more emotionally literate too. A rigidly enforced dress code ensured none of them came to work dressed as if for a nightclub. This kept things on a professional basis for everyone.

Although he had always desired marriage for the respectability and stability it afforded, he had never expected to meet someone to whom he could make that commitment. He had never imagined meeting a woman who could straddle both camps.

That night in California when he had got to know the real Rosa, the woman under the starchy surface, he had been delighted to discover someone with an easy wit to match her quick brain. Her understated attractiveness had blossomed. She would, he had realised, make boring corporate functions tolerable without clinging like a limpet to his arm.

Best of all, she was vehemently against emotional entanglements. He had come to suspect that in Rosa, as in himself, that particular gene had been switched off.

But even emotionally illiterate people had physical needs. Rosa was no exception.

And neither was he.

The blossoming he had first spotted in California had now flowered into a sexy radiance of creamy skin hidden by far too much material. Soon, he vowed, Rosa would unpeel the clothing covering her delectable body and reveal herself to his willing, devouring eyes. And then he would devour her.

'There are a couple of things I want to correct you on,' he

said, his voice throaty. 'I do *not* regard my female employees as "drones". They are simply my employees, and they are afforded the respect they deserve for the quality of their work and not their gender.'

'Good comeback.' She nodded approvingly and raised her glass, taking another long drink through her straw.

'One other correction in your assessment.' He leaned across the table and dropped his voice, forcing her to lean closer so she could hear him. 'I *do* desire you, Mrs Baranski. And I would love nothing more than the opportunity to prove it.'

Rosa scowled and leaned back, folding her arms across her chest. 'Why do you have to spoil it? We were having a lovely conversation…'

'Discussing my faults?' he interjected.

'Absolutely.' She nodded. 'As I said, we were having a lovely conversation and you had to reduce it to a basic level.'

'Your cheeks are burning.'

'Thanks for pointing that out.'

'Do I make you hot?'

'Shut up.'

'You make *me* hot.'

'The only thing hot about you is the air that comes out of your mouth.'

'So harsh.' He sighed. 'And such a lie too.' Before she could splutter with outrage, he grinned. 'Shall we make it the best of three games?'

'Only if you promise to stop talking about sex.'

Once they had taken seven tiles each, he could not resist pressing her a little further. 'What do you think about making this game more interesting?'

'How?'

'If either of us gets a triple letter word the other has to remove an item of clothing.'

'You'd be naked in two goes.'

'One.'

'Oh…'

'Feeling hot again?' he purred, noting the colour of her neck.

'If you make one more lewd remark I'm abandoning the game.'

'Then I will win by default.'

Her pursed lips loosened, a smile beginning to crack out of all that sternness. 'You always have to get the last word in.'

He grinned again. As much as she tried to deny it, Rosa's immunity to him was weakening by the minute. He was scratching under the surface of her skin and piercing into the delicious flesh. Soon she would be his for the taking.

Her eyes narrowed, a shrewdness flickering in them. 'I'll make a deal with you. If I win this game you are not to talk about sex for the rest of the holiday.'

'And if *I* win?'

'If you win I'll get some earplugs.'

'I'll agree to one night—if you win I promise I will not talk about sex again until tomorrow morning.'

'That includes innuendo.'

'You have a deal.'

This would be an easy win. Rosa had played two games of Scrabble. She had picked it up quickly, but he had gone easy on her on the basis it was unfair to humiliate a novice. Not this time.

'When I win I can talk about sex all night if I so wish. I can tell you exactly what I would like to do with your ravishing body, how I spend inordinate amounts of time wondering what colour your nipples are and what they taste like…'

'Stop it.' Rosa's protest came out as a moan. The second he had mentioned her nipples she had become wholly conscious of how sensitised they had become—as her whole being had become. Her skin was almost dancing with awareness.

Listening to his gravelly voice purring the words in Russian, she had felt the blood in her system heating to unbearable levels.

She crossed her legs, as if the act could smother the pulsations between her thighs, and forced her voice to sound at least reasonably normal. 'You play dirty.'

His green eyes glittered. 'I like dirty. I especially like playing dirty with husky-voiced bombshells.'

He was impossible to talk to!

Growling under her breath, Rosa pulled a letter out from the green sack. 'Typical.' She had pulled out the letter X.

Naturally Nico pulled out a B. He didn't even try to hide his smirk. 'I shall start, then.'

It became immediately apparent that he was set on winning. All dirty talk stopped, and his focus was solely on the letters lined up in front of him.

Of course as soon as it was her turn the innuendoes started again.

'Stop trying to put me off,' she complained after her third move. He was already forty points ahead. 'That's bad sportsmanship.'

He smirked, although his eyes were creased in concentration. 'If you can't take the heat...'

'I should jump into the pool.'

'Sorry?'

'If I can't take the heat I should jump into the swimming pool.' She smiled in what she hoped was a seductive manner, suddenly compelled to give him a taste of his own medicine. She was making it too easy for him. Why should she be the only one to suffer? 'Maybe I should jump into the pool naked?'

Not taking her eyes off him, she slowly closed her lips around her straw and sucked.

'You are playing with fire,' he warned, grabbing the wrist holding the straw.

'Really?' She adopted a surprised look. 'We're only talking. If you would prefer I stop talking you only have to say. And then shut up too.'

He shook his head with incredulity before grazing a kiss across her knuckles. 'Game on.'

She blinked at the unexpected intimacy, but forced her mind to concentrate.

His next move took him eighty-three points clear.

Rosa had no intention of going down without a fight, but it was a lot harder than it should have been. Nico had dropped the verbal flirtation, but whenever it was her turn he would fix those green eyes on her and seduce her with them—at least until the sun got into them and he started squinting.

'That'll teach you,' she sniggered, placing three tiles on the board and clawing back thirty much needed points.

The game progressed slowly. As hard as she tried, she couldn't quite catch him, only able to shave off a few points here and there. She was twenty-six points behind when she removed the final tiles from the bag.

For an age Nico's face was scrunched in concentration. He took a sip of his cocktail, his eyes meeting hers with a look that could only be described as triumphant. Slowly, deliberately, he placed six of his tiles on the board.

'I think you'll find that comes to sixty-two points which puts me eighty-eight points ahead with only one tile left.'

Ouch!

'Do you want to admit defeat?'

'No chance.' She frowned and stared at her letters, waiting for them to magically form a super-duper...

Ha!

How she kept her face poker straight she would never know, but, after positioning her S at the bottom of Nico's last-laid word, she placed all her tiles on the board. 'I think you'll find that comes to thirty-six points, plus a bonus fifty points for using all my letters.'

The smirk playing on his lips vanished. Quickly he made his own calculations.

'So it's down to your last tile,' she observed. 'Let's have a look.'

With obvious reluctance he picked it up and held his palm open. It was a C, worth three points which would be deducted from his total and added to hers.

'Would it be in really bad taste for me to jump up and down and squeal like a banshee?' she asked.

'Yes.'

'Thought so.' She got to her feet. 'I can be gracious in victory. Seeing as you lost, you can pack the board away. I'm going for a shower—all this heat is getting to me. See you later, loser.'

Still sniggering, she went straight to the *en suite* bathroom and locked the door behind her.

Rosa had to give Nico credit—he'd stopped sulking by the time their evening meal was served. At least she assumed he had been sulking, seeing as he had whiled away the last hours of the afternoon in the saloon.

As the heat of the day had barely been dented, they decided to eat on the sundeck, consuming a bottle of chilled white wine with their meal.

'Is this what people do on holiday?' she asked, once she had cleared her coconut mousse with a contented sigh. 'Laze about doing not very much and consuming lots of alcohol? And not to forget beating their spouse at Scrabble?'

His lips quirked. 'Tomorrow I will teach you to play chess.'

'Sounds exciting.'

'You will need all your concentration.'

'I'm sure I'll cope.'

'Same rules as today?'

She pondered. 'Best of three—but no flirting or innuendo *at all* during play. Deal?'

He extended a hand. 'If we are going to make a deal we must seal it with a handshake.'

I'd much rather seal it with a kiss, she thought, before checking herself. Time to cut back on the alcohol. Her thoughts were becoming extremely wayward, running further away with every look at him. And, really, Nico *did* look stunningly handsome under the moonlight. More so than normal, which she had not thought possible. Somehow he made a pair of knee-length shorts and a green polo-shirt look sexy.

Surreptitiously wiping her palm on her skirt first, she took his hand, expecting a quick shake and then release.

Nico clasped his fingers over hers, pulling her hand close so he could examine it. 'Your hands are tiny,' he said, holding his hand to hers.

'I am half your size,' she commented, with a nonchalance that belied the swirls of heat pervading through her. To cover her nervous excitement she downed the rest of her wine.

'Tell me why you have never taken a holiday before,' he said, still gazing at her hand.

'There's nothing to tell. The opportunity was never there.' Why had she not snatched her hand away? And why had her heartbeat trebled, with pulses of excitement hopping across her skin?

'But you earn good money. It's not as if you can't afford it.'

'I've always had better things to spend my money on.'

'Such as?'

'Education. Rent and then mortgage. Food, fancy shoes and handbags. You know—the usual.'

'I know it well.'

He raised his eyes to meet hers. The intensity whirling in them had an effect that was almost hypnotic.

'Did your father ever take you on holiday—it *was* just you and your father, wasn't it?'

'Yes, it was just me and my father. And, no, we never went on holiday.' Nico released her hand and finished his wine. 'Coffee?'

'Please.'

The hand he'd released tingled so much she rammed it between her thighs, glad the moonlight prevented him from seeing the colour blazing across her neck and face.

He pressed the intercom and spoke quietly into it, all the while keeping his eyes fixed on her.

Past history was not something they had discussed. When they had decided to marry right there and then in California, she had asked if his parents would be disappointed not to attend. He had shaken his head.

'My mother died when I was a toddler,' he had said, as collected as always. 'And my father isn't a man for ceremony.'

It had not been mentioned or alluded to since by either of them.

Why was that?

How could you spend eleven months living with someone and know next to nothing about them other than how they took their coffee?

She had been too scared to ask. Not scared of Nico's reaction to any probing questions, but scared of *her* reaction. Sharing histories had felt an intimacy too far—way beyond the remit of their marriage pact.

But now, with the moonlight beaming above and a slight breeze tempering the warm glow from all the wine she'd consumed, it all seemed so irrelevant. She enjoyed Nico's company, she found him incredibly sexy—why not take the opportunity to get to know him better while she still had the chance? What did she have to lose?

Once their plates had been cleared and the coffee delivered, Rosa placed her elbows on the table and rested her chin on her hands, admiring the graceful way he poured the dark brown liquid. For such a large man there was an elegance about his movements she found more and more captivating.

'What was it like, growing up in Siberia?'

'Cold.'

'Hilarious. I'm curious, though—what *was* it like? Whenever I think of Siberia all I can think of is *Dr Zhivago*.'

'*Dr Zhivago* was written seventy years ago.'

'Exactly. Incidentally, it is my favourite book. But I am curious to know what it's really like.'

Nico poured a splash of milk into his cup. 'Why do you want to know?'

'Sheer curiosity. You're the one who said we should use this time to get to know each other better,' she reminded him pointedly. 'Unless you were only saying that in the hope I would drop my knickers?'

He looked up at her, his lips twitching, his eyes gleaming. He took a sip of the hot liquid. 'I lived in a small mining town. I cannot talk for the rest of Siberia because I never visited it.'

'What was your town like?'

'Small and boring. I learned to make my own amusements.'

'Did your father ever remarry?'

'No.'

'Did he ever come close?'

'No.'

'Why not?'

'I have no idea. I would imagine the dearth of women had something to do with it.'

'Why was there a dearth of women?'

'The town is in one of Siberia's remotest regions. The sum-

mers aren't too bad but the winters are cruel and long. There
are very few families and most of them move on when their
children reach school age.'

'Were there any children your age?'

'There were a couple of older boys I was educated with.'

'What about girls?'

'Girls?'

'You know—the humans with the x and y chromosomes.'

'It was the families with girls who got out the quickest. It
was a man's town.'

'That must have been hard for you,' she observed, feeling a pang for the child Nico had been, cut off from the rest
of civilisation with only a couple of friends and no female
figure in his life.

He shrugged. 'It was my life. I knew no different.'

'But something must have made you want to leave it.'

'Books. My father is a voracious reader. He encouraged me
to read so I would learn that our town was only a tiny atom in
the world. He was determined his life would not be my life.'

Rosa's throat closed.

So they did have something in common other than a ten-
dency towards workaholicism. Books. The need for escape.
The knowledge that the hands they had been dealt did not
have to define them for all eternity.

'Why did he not leave when you were a child, like the
other families?'

'My father is a functioning alcoholic,' he stated flatly. 'He's
the only drunk I've ever met who drinks his way through a
bar with a book in his hand. Any hopes or ambitions were
subverted by the bottom of a bottle.'

'Not all of them,' she countered, her heart in her throat.
Nico had been raised by an alcoholic? Oh, the poor, poor
child. 'He had hopes and ambitions for *you*.'

His eyes still held hers, but the light contained in them had been snuffed out. 'Those ambitions were not of the present. He would come home drunk in the middle of the night—I would be awake, waiting to make sure he had walked back safely—and tell me that he wanted a different life for me. He would say that if I worked hard and studied hard I would be able to leave the town and do anything I wanted.'

'He was right.'

'Yes, he was right,' he conceded. 'And it would sound idyllic—except he would be delivering these drunken lectures after I had spent the day taking myself to school and back, washing, cleaning and feeding myself because there was no thought in his head of doing those things for me.'

Rosa's eyes widened. 'You had to fend for yourself?'

'Always. I do not remember it ever being different.' He laughed mirthlessly. 'I could build a fire at five and was given housekeeping money when I was seven.'

Witnessing the horror in Rosa's eyes, Nico wished he could take back his words. He didn't even know why he was revealing so much. It was those damn unwavering eyes of hers. They contained far too much warmth. A man could throw himself into that swirling caramel if he wasn't careful.

'It wasn't as bad as I am making it sound,' he retracted, feeling an inordinate amount of guilt at his disloyalty. His father was not a bad man—something he had recognised even as a small child. 'There was an elderly woman who lived quite close by. I think she felt sorry for me. Sometimes she would bring a pot of stew to our house. She would never come in. Just leave it on the doorstep.'

Even now, decades on, he could still taste that stew. Even now, decades on, having dined in the world's finest restaurants and been catered for by the world's finest chefs, he had never tasted anything as good.

'My father took care of me as best he could,' he explained

quietly, not sure why he felt the need to make her understand, only knowing he did not want Rosa to think badly of the man who had raised him. 'I know that by today's standards he neglected me, but I never felt it. I am certain if I had not been around he would have drunk himself into an early grave.'

Rosa's hand covered his—just a light pressure, but enough to sear his skin.

'You do not need to explain your father to me, Nico,' she said, staring at him with eyes that contained a mixture of pity and...was that *envy*? Surely not? 'It took guts for him to keep you. He must love you very much.'

He wanted to move his hand, snatch it away, but the warmth transmuted from her skin acted like glue, binding them together.

Nico did not want her sympathy, or empathy, or whatever it was seeping from her. All he wanted was to hear her throaty laugh and watch those caramel eyes darken into chocolate as he took possession of her.

He could not remove his hand.

The easy, yet sexually charged atmosphere that had been swirling between them for days had tightened. The air was so thick it almost resembled a misty fog.

But this was so much more than mere sexual tension.

What the hell was he doing? He was supposed to be laying the path to seduction, not unbuttoning about things that rarely passed from his lips.

Slowly, he pulled his hand away. He wanted her hands to rest on him in passion, not sympathy.

'After my mother died of pneumonia my father had a duty to raise me.'

'But he could have absolved himself from that responsibility,' she contradicted with a flick of her ponytail.

'My father, for all his faults, would never have absolved himself from his responsibilities.'

'Then he is a better man than a lot of parents.'

It was on the tip of his tongue to ask what her comment meant, to probe the reason for the clouding of those eyes. But he did not want to hear it. Getting to know each other better did not mean learning each other's intimate secrets. The only intimacy he wanted from Rosa was in the bedroom.

He flashed a grin. 'It's getting late. Fancy a game of Scrabble before bed?'

Rosa did not trust Nico's grin. It was too...*fake*—as if he were a marionette having its strings pulled.

She could understand that. While he had defended his father, and in her mind it was evident his father had loved him, there was no escaping the fact that Nico's childhood had been harsh. Sometimes the past was too painful to talk about.

Some confidences were a confidence too far.

'If it's all the same to you, I think I'll go to bed.' She got to her feet and flashed a grin she knew looked every bit as fake as his. 'I'm all Scrabbled out.'

Nico's answering smile relieved some of the oppressive tension that had enveloped them, allowing her to breathe a little easier. 'Is this the part where you get some barbed wire and roll it down the centre of the bed?'

'Gosh, not only are you supremely intelligent and a whizz at making money, but you can read minds. Are there no limits to your talents?'

'None that I have discovered.'

'And so incredibly modest. Goodnight.'

'I'll be joining you soon.'

'Don't rush on my account. Go and find the crew. Watch the sun come up with them.'

His low chuckles followed her all the way into the suite.

CHAPTER EIGHT

IN THE *EN SUITE* bathroom, Rosa stripped down to her knickers, splashed water onto her face and cleaned her teeth. The skin that had been exposed to the sun had pinkened, and she wrinkled her slightly burned nose. Why couldn't her skin turn a lovely golden hue?

Nico had beautiful golden skin.

She blew out a puff of air. She really did not want to be reminded of his fantastic physique—not when she would shortly be sharing a bed with him. It had been bad enough spending the day with his gorgeous chest parked in her eyeline. There had been more than one occasion when she had wanted to yell at him to put a T-shirt on. But she had known perfectly well how he would react to that and had wisely kept her mouth shut.

A shiver ran through her. Would he keep to his side of their earlier wager?

Nico was a man of his word, she reminded herself. The chances of him reneging on it and starting a whole load of sex talk as she fell into slumber were extremely remote.

The thought made her feel surprisingly flat. Could that really be disappointment?

Lord knew how she would react if he *did* renege. Hopefully she would have the presence of mind to put a sock in his mouth. If her reaction from earlier was any indication, though, she would be a puddling wreck within seconds.

It was too unfair. Why did he have to possess a voice that was more molten than lava? Why could he not have some dreadful nasally whine, whereby dirty talk sounded ridiculous?

But then, Nico didn't even have to speak. Just thinking about him was becoming enough to turn her into a puddling wreck.

She felt as if she had learned more about him in a day than she had in the whole time she had worked for him and been married to him. His refusal to blame his father for such a harsh childhood, his attempts to mitigate it, humanised him, stripped back the layers to reveal the man beneath the towering powerhouse shell.

She forced herself to look at her reflection. Was she really so different from his usual lovers?

The answer was a resounding *yes*. Unless she was strapped to a stretching machine for a year and had a bucket of bleach tipped over her head she could never look like those lithe beauties. She'd probably need a nose-job too.

How could she trust that he really did want her for herself and not out of revenge? If he had an inkling of why she had slept with Stephen...

And how could she trust her own feelings around him? He had confided a part of his past to her and it had felt as if a stack of knives were ripping into her heart.

She had wanted to climb onto his lap and wrap her arms around him.

In all the years she had been with Stephen she had never felt that urge towards him—not even when his grandmother had died. She had hated herself for her coldness but she had not been able to cross that breach.

The last time she recalled giving physical comfort, she had

been in her early teens. A young girl, newly orphaned, had been brought into the care home whilst foster care was arranged for her. She had been placed in Rosa's dormitory for the night. Rosa had heard the devastated child whimpering in her sleep and had crawled into her bed. She had held the child in her arms, stroked her hair and soothed her until she had finally fallen asleep, clinging onto Rosa like a limpet.

The next morning the girl had left. Rosa had never seen her again. Over the years she had often thought of her, had often prayed the child had found a new family who loved and cherished her.

Hearing the patio doors to the decking area close, she blinked the past away and hurriedly donned the only suitable clothing she had found that could be used as nightwear.

She breezed past Nico and turned over the sheets on the bed. 'Is there a preference for which side you like to sleep?' she asked politely.

'Your side,' he said, his lips twitching.

'Not going to happen.'

'Can't blame a man for trying. By the way, what are you *wearing*?'

'This old thing?' She looked down at the cotton shirt that reached below her knees. 'Just something I found in your dressing room.'

'You've been going through my clothes?'

'I would apologise—but a), you went through my clothing at some point to get my dress size, and b), you didn't bother to arrange a decent set of pyjamas for me. There's no way on earth I'm going to wear those scraps of lace I assume are supposed to be nightwear.'

And no way was she going to admit that she had gazed at them for an inordinate amount of time, wondering what it would be like to wear such sexy, exotic apparel.

'So you thought you would help yourself to one of my shirts?'

'Got a problem with that?' she asked, raising a brow in challenge.

His eyes sparkled. 'I happen to think you look incredibly sexy in my shirt.

'Oh, go away.'

Chuckling, he disappeared into the *en suite*.

Rosa flopped onto her back and gazed up at the ceiling. When she had pilfered his shirt she had felt a sense of vindication at getting herself out of a pickle. Now the heat cresting through her made her wonder if she should have stuck to a pair of knickers and a T-shirt. Except the T-shirts in the dressing room were all tiny designer numbers that would cover her shoulders but not much else.

She had thought half a bottle of wine would send her into an immediate slumber, and silently cursed herself for having coffee.

Much as she tried to keep her mind occupied, away from any errant thoughts about what Nico might be doing in the bathroom and what state of undress he might be in, she was all too aware of the shower running.

She forced her mind to concentrate on anything but Nico, determined not to think of him naked, lathering under the steaming water. Anything would do. The economy. The pink designer shoes she had spotted on Bond Street.

She might as well tell herself not to think about purple elephants.

Grimacing, she forced herself to take deep breaths before jumping off the bed and helping herself to a bottle of water from the discreetly placed fridge.

She was getting back into bed when the bathroom door opened and Nico appeared, wearing nothing but a tiny towel across his snake hips. A waft of warm, citrusy steam fol-

lowed in his wake and she sucked in a breath, moisture filling her mouth.

His black hair was damp, his golden skin a deeper bronze
after a day of glorious sunshine. Seriously, had there *ever*
been a finer specimen of the male form? He was truly magnificent—a Roman statue brought to life.

And, no matter how dispassionately she tried to see him,
her body seemed to go into some form of meltdown. Could
he not just *put some bloody clothes on*?

He looked at her and raised a brow.

'Please don't tell me I said that aloud?' she begged.

'Do you have a problem with my body?' he asked, with
the arrogant look of one who knew his form was damn near
perfect.

'Only when you're not wearing clothes.' That was a lie.
She had a problem with him clothed too. But near-as-dammit
naked…?

'Why? What is wrong with me?'

'Nothing.' And that was the precise problem.

Rosa had never considered herself a shallow person, but
right then she wished he had a massive paunch and a hairy
back. Anything had to be better than the reality, which was
that she wanted nothing more than to run her fingers through
the black silken hair covering his broad, muscular chest and
taste his smooth skin.

Just like that, her belly flipped, and heat went rampaging
through her blood. For a moment she stood paralysed, treacle-
thick desire rooting her to the floor.

The beautiful golden chest in front of her eyes rose sharply.
As if drawn by a magnet, she looked up, Meeting his gaze,
she sucked in a breath.

The intensity in those green eyes…

Dear God, if she had wanted proof he really did desire her
for herself, and not out of some stupid game or pride, it was

there, resonating out of him—as pure and tangible a desire as she had ever seen.

The very air around them thickened. Heat was licking her bones, flowing low, deep into her pelvis, forming a physical ache in her core.

Every inch of her felt alive, as if she could feel the charge of every electron ever created on her skin. And her breasts...

Not since they had first started to develop had she been so aware of them. Without looking down she knew the nipples had puckered, were straining against the fabric of his shirt.

'Do you have a problem with me sleeping naked next to you?'

A problem? Yes, she would say she had a problem with that—the problem being her own desire to strip his shirt off and get naked with him.

'I think it would be gentlemanly for you to wear a pair of shorts,' she said, the words coming from a throat that felt ragged.

'Your wish is my command.' Turning his back to her, thus giving her an excellent view of his lean torso from behind and endless muscular legs, he stepped briefly into the dressing room, returning with a pair of black undershorts in his hand. 'Will these suffice?'

She swallowed. 'They'll do.'

Rosa realised she had been gawping at him like a hormone-filled teenager and hurriedly climbed back under the silk bedsheets, nestling into them like a cocoon, pretending not to be aware of Nico dropping his towel and stepping into the undershorts. She would not peek. No way. She would keep her eyes tightly closed.

The bed dipped.

She squeezed her eyes even tighter. Blocking her senses made a whole heap of sense.

The bed was huge, but she could still feel the heat from his body permeating through the sheets. It dipped again as Nico reached for the row of switches on the wall behind them and turned the lights off.

Rosa shivered as they were plunged into darkness. 'Could you keep the bathroom light on, please?'

After he'd fiddled with the switches, the suite was filled with a muted glow from the *en suite* bathroom.

'Thank you.'

'I didn't know you were afraid of the dark.' Nico said.

'I'm not,' she lied, keeping her back firmly to him, 'I just prefer to sleep with a light on. Goodnight.'

'Don't I get a goodnight kiss?'

'No. Go to sleep.'

Nico listened to Rosa's breathing—a deep, rhythmic sound that was strangely comforting. Such a different sound from the noisy snore that would reverberate throughout the small wooden house he had shared with his father. At times Nico had been quite certain the house would collapse from the drunken sound. Despite the noise being reminiscent of a pneumatic drill, he had taken comfort from it. It had meant his father was alive.

Self-sufficiency was not something he had been born with. It was a trait he had learned through necessity. Until he had left home for university in Moscow it had been just him and his father. In his dreams he still felt the terror he had known as a small child, when he would lie in bed night after night, praying to whoever was looking out for his father that he'd be brought home safely. And he did come home. Every night. No matter how deep his stupor, his father had never forgotten he had a son at home, waiting for him. Waiting for him with the light on.

Why did Rosa need a light on?

He rubbed his fingers into his temples, trying to eradicate

the question, the answer to which he had no business know-ing. The only intimacy he wanted from Rosa was physical. Nothing more. The fact he had already revealed a little of himself earlier was cause for alarm. He could have answered her questions without going into detail. Which begged the question: why hadn't he?

The past was aptly named. Learn from history and move on, taking those lessons into the future but not dwelling on them.

Nico had learned that lesson well.

Naturally he had tried every trick in the book to get his father to straighten out, even going as far as to book him into an alcohol treatment facility in America that was reputed to be one of the toughest in the world. That was the day his fa-ther had taken him to one side.

'Nicolai, I cannot allow you to spend any more money on me. These people will not cure me.'

'How do you know that?' he had demanded. 'These people are the best at dealing with chronic alcoholics.'

'But, Nicolai, I do not want to be cured.' He had fixed re-markably clear, sober eyes onto him. 'If it were not for you I would have died a long time ago. Please, my son, stop try-ing. I do not want to meet reality.'

That was when he had realised it was pointless trying to save a man who did not want to be saved. All he could do was try and provide as safe an environment as possible for his father to pickle himself in.

Now Nico had the peace of mind knowing his father was in a warm home, with assistance at the press of a button. No more staggering over a mile every night in knee-deep snow and blizzards; his father lived in a ground floor apartment in Moscow, with a choice of bars within a short walk and a small army of unobtrusive carers ready to scoop him up if he should fall. He also had the comfort of knowing his father was a sociable drunk. He might not want to talk to anyone, but at least he preferred to drink with other humans around him.

His mind drifted to the picture of his mother he kept in his wallet. One of only a handful of pictures of Katerina Baranski left, it resided in the back of his wallet, rarely looked at, rarely thought about. But it was always there, always with him. How different would his life have been if she had lived beyond his second birthday?

Rosa sighed in her sleep, the muted sound a welcome distraction. Ruminating on the past was pointless. He turned his face to stare at her back, as stiff as a rod even in slumber. Only the top of her ebony hair was poking out beneath the cocoon of blankets she had made for herself.

Did Rosa have a picture of her parents in her wallet?

He felt a sharp pang in his chest. At least his father was still alive. Rosa had no one.

Rubbing his hand down his face, he closed his eyes.

He needed to get some sleep. His mind was all over the place, heading into dangerous territory.

The sooner the sun came up the better. Then he could advance his seduction of her and find some peace in knowing his marriage was intact.

The bed dipped.

Rosa's eyes snapped open.

Sitting at the foot of the bed, tray in hand, was Nico.

'I bring you breakfast,' he said, flashing his white teeth at her.

'What time is it?' she asked, placing a hand over her mouth to smother a yawn.

'Nine o'clock.'

She groaned and squeezed her eyes shut. It still felt like the middle of the night.

As ridiculous as she knew it to be, she had spent the night

rooted to the spot, not quite at the edge of the bed, too scared to move. Her limbs ached from being forced to remain in the same position for hours on end.

No matter how hard she'd tried, she had been unable to relax. She had been far too aware of the warm body lying mere feet away from her. Every time she had dozed off Nico's scent had wafted under her nose, yanking her right back into consciousness.

'Come on, lazy bones, sit up. Your breakfast is getting cold.'

It took a few moments, but somehow she managed to disentangle herself from the sheets that had smothered her all night and hoik herself upright. Now she was moving blood moved freely back to her limbs, which were all screaming obscenities at her.

'Have you been working out?' she asked, noting the sheen of perspiration soaking through his white T-shirt. He used their home gym regularly, but jogging was his preferred form of exercise. She guessed being stuck in the middle of the ocean limited his options for a good run.

'I have,' he said, placing the tray on her lap and removing the silver lid from the plate to reveal poached eggs on toast. A bowl of fruit and a glass of orange juice were placed next to it. He got to his feet. 'Coffee?'

'Yes, please.' She rubbed at her neck before taking a drink of the orange juice, which went some way to soothing her arid throat.

'Is your neck hurting again?'

She pulled a face.

'Would you like me to rub it better for you?'

'Would you like me to stab you with my fork?' Not taking her eyes off him, she stabbed it into an egg.

Amusement played on his lips. 'I have a weapon I can assault you with if you are so inclined.'

'Don't start,' she said, shaking her head. 'It's too early for innuendoes.'

'Our deal only lasted for a night,' he reminded her with a lopsided grin. 'You're now officially fair game.'

'Not until we've done three rounds of chess.' She winced as she felt another sharp twinge in her neck.

'It's hardly surprising you're having neck problems with the way you sleep,' Nico said, resting his arms back and openly studying her with his gorgeous green eyes. 'It was like sleeping next to a mannequin. Tell me—do all women sleep as if they are encased in concrete?'

'You should know—you've slept with enough of us.' She popped some egg and toast into her mouth.

'I have never slept with a woman in my life.'

Rosa stopped chewing and eyed him with suspicion. Swallowing the food, she almost choked. 'Nico, you have slept with *loads* of women.'

'That is inaccurate. I have never actually slept with a woman before.'

'Rubbish. You've slept with more women then I have digits and limbs. And eyes. And—'

'No.' He cut her off with an amused frown. 'I have had sex with a number of women, but I have never slept with any of them.'

She could not hide her incredulity. 'Seriously? You've never fallen asleep with a woman before?'

'I find women like cuddles after sex.' He spoke as if *cuddles* were a dirty word. 'But that is not for me.'

'What do you do, then?' she asked, horrified and fascinated all at once. 'Kick them out of bed the second you've come? Or do you come and run?' She laughed at her own joke, anything to hide the sickening churn of her stomach.

'It's not quite as sordid as you're trying to make out. I have never invited a woman into my bed, so that situation has never arisen. I simply thank them for a great evening and leave.'

'Ooh, what a gentleman you are. You really know how to make a woman feel special.'

'Is it not better than leading them on?'

The amusement in his eyes had dimmed a little, the intensity increasing. She had the strangest feeling he was trying to convey a message to her.

'I make it clear from the outset that I am not offering any sort of permanency. If I were to stick around afterwards and whisper endearments I would be lying and offering a false promise. I do not make false promises, Rosa, but neither do I set out to humiliate them. They know the score from the beginning. It's just sex. Nothing more, nothing less.'

She continued to meet his stare whilst chewing another forkful of egg, struggling to work out what he was trying to tell her.

Before she could ask he raised an arm and sniffed. 'I'd better have a shower before I start to smell.' He rose to his feet with his usual languid grace. 'Finish your breakfast. When you're dressed and ready, I'll give you a good thrashing at chess. Before I forget, you might want to put on a higher factor sun cream today—the Captain tells me it is going to be a scorcher.'

Thoroughly confused, she watched him retreat into the *en suite* bathroom.

The more she recalled his words, the more her brain became befuddled. Was it a warning or an explanation? Was he telling her that, even though he wanted to sleep with her, she was not to expect anything more? Or was he trying to tell her what his attitude *had* been?

She took a sip of her coffee and forced herself to think coherently.

Nico wanted their marriage to continue. He had spelt that

out more than once. He wanted their marriage to be a proper one. With sex.

Could she really do it? Could she really give herself to him? Because one thing was clear—if she were to give her husband her body, there was every danger she would give so much more with it.

CHAPTER NINE

'WHY DON'T YOU leave your hair loose?' Nico asked when Rosa joined him on the sundeck. As usual she had scraped it back into a tight ponytail.

'Because it's a pain in the bum and keeps getting in my eyes.' She took the seat opposite him and frowned down at the carved figures laid out in their respective starting positions.

'You have such beautiful hair. It's a shame you don't let it free.'

The simple sincerity in his voice reached inside her and knocked off a fragment of the wall surrounding her heart. She almost heard it smash. Her hands shaking, she tightened her hair further.

He smiled ruefully, pushing a piece of paper to her. 'I've written out what all the pieces are and the moves they can make. Have a read of it while I make us some cocktails.'

'Already?' She blinked and looked at her watch. 'It's not even eleven o'clock yet.'

'We're on holiday,' he said, as if that explained everything.

'And this is what people do on holiday?'

'Rosa, a holiday is a time to relax—and let your hair down,' he added with a smirk. 'Soon you will get into the swing of it.'

She gazed around at the gleaming ocean and the cobalt blue of the sky and sighed with pleasure. 'I never realised how wonderful it was to do nothing.'

'It is strange, yes?'

Although his eyes were covered with sunglasses, she could feel his gaze resting upon her.

'Yes,' she agreed, knowing exactly what he meant. 'It is a little strange.'

'You will get used to it. And when you do, you will re-alise regular breaks are essential to keep your brain firing on all cylinders.' He paused, a sensuous look flittering over his face. 'Do you know what would make you relax even more?'

Inexplicably, her mouth went dry. She shook her head.

'A massage. I think we should change the terms of our deal. I don't mean to sound superior, but there is little chance of you beating me at chess. If I win three games in row, I get to give you a full-body massage.'

'And that is supposed to be my forfeit?' Was that dry croak really her voice?

He removed his glasses, hitting her with the full power of his magnetic stare. 'No *daragaya*, that is to be my prize.'

After a beat, he rose.

'You can give me your answer when I return. I suggest you read through the moves while I am gone.'

Rosa watched him stroll away, her heart pounding errati-cally against her ribs. Idly she fingered the piece of paper and, despite the churning that was threatening to consume her whole, found her attention caught by the intricate sketches Nico had drawn to represent each piece. She had often no-ticed the strength of his hands and the dexterity of his long, capable fingers...

A thrill ran up her spine as she considered what it would be like to have those proficient fingers kneading her flesh, touching her...

Dear God, she should be dismissing his suggestion out of hand, but...

It felt as she had spent eleven months climbing in a very

slow, very steep rollercoaster, her anticipation and fear increasing the higher the carriage climbed. Now she had reached the top and could see the fall coming, but was helpless to get off—helpless to find the reverse button that would take her back to safety. There was nothing to stop gravity taking its course and plunging her over the top.

Think of the exhilaration of the ride.

But think of the consequences should the carriage come off the track.

Absently she kneaded the back of her aching neck.

'Thinking about what it would feel like to have me massage all that tension out of your system?'

Nico's voice broke her out of her tortured reverie. Her eyes flew to him. He was carrying a pitcher of light green liquid and two glasses, evoking an enormous sense of *déjà vu*. Which was not surprising, seeing as he had performed the same action only twenty-four hours before.

Yet twenty-four hours ago she had hardly dared allow herself to think about sleeping with him, too fearful of the powerful feelings such a thought provoked. Now...? Now the burn inside her, the ache... Now she didn't know if she even *wanted* to control it any more.

Nico was trying to create a proper marriage for them and she was letting fear block it. Surely it was time to step out of the shackles of the past and place her faith in a man she was already halfway to falling in love with?

Love?

She didn't even know what it was. Not really.

Love was a word bandied about too much.

Her mother had professed to love her. And then she had abandoned her.

She had taken her foster mother into her heart only to be rejected.

Stephen had professed to love her, but he wouldn't even let

her *breathe*. With Stephen she had always kept the essence of herself hidden, rigidly maintaining her barriers. He'd never even come close to breaking through.

With Nico those same barriers were crumbling. The foundations were shaking. Everything was conspiring to pull the last of her fortress down—the sun, the setting and most especially Nico. Everything about him awoke senses she hadn't been aware existed. He made her *feel*.

She straightened her spine and looked him square in the eyes. 'Yes. I have been thinking about that.'

He merely raised an eyebrow. 'And?'

Sometimes he was just too cool for school.

She picked up her glass and took a sip, then used her middle finger to slowly wipe the residue away from her mouth. 'And the answer is yes.'

His eyes gleamed with a vibrancy that made the breath catch in her throat. He held his glass aloft. 'To us.'

She chinked her glass to his. 'To us,' she echoed, striving vainly to match his collectedness.

A long, charged pause settled between them before he said, 'To make it more of a competition, I will remove three of my pawns for each of the games.'

'You're not worried I might pick it up as well as I picked up Scrabble?' she could not resist asking, her voice huskier than usual.

He shook his head. 'Chess is a game of strategy. It takes years of practice to become proficient at it. My father taught me to play when I was a young boy so I have decades on you.'

'How young?'

'Five.'

'Crikey. That *is* young.' Automatically her thoughts flew to her own childhood, to being five years old. That was *the* most vivid age in her early memories. How could it not be?

It was the age she been ripped away from everything and everyone she loved.

She pushed the maudlin thoughts away. She was twenty-seven years old and had spent her entire life trying to be a good girl, trying to do the right thing. She had convinced herself that if she behaved one day her mother would come back and get her.

Her mother had never come back. She hadn't wanted her. And when, at the age of eight, she had finally been approved as a candidate for adoption: no one else had wanted her either.

She had spent the rest of her life pushing everyone away because of it.

She wanted Nico with a desperate, hungry craving she could no longer control. And he wanted her too.

He was right. They could be good together. But they would never know unless she took a chance.

Was she really prepared to risk what could be a happy future for them because of fear?

No. Not any more.

Today would be the next turning point in her life.

Today the barriers would come down.

She was in charge of her own destiny. That destiny was with Nico. She just had to trust…

Filling her lungs to stave off the nervous butterflies playing inside her chest, she placed her fingers at the hem of her T-shirt and slowly pulled it up, past her belly, past her bikini-covered breasts, and over her head.

Done, she locked eyes with him and felt an enormous thrill of power and excitement surge through her.

Nico took a long gulp of his cocktail.

'It's very hot,' she commented, in the most matter-of-fact voice she could muster.

'*Da.*'

If his eyes were any wider she figured they might just pop out of his head.

'I think I will take my shorts off too.'

Keeping her eyes fixed firmly on his stunned face, she stood up. She undid the button, then teased the zip loose and wriggled the shorts down her hips and thighs before letting them fall in a puddle at her ankles. Casually she stepped out of them and bent over to pick them up from the floor.

'You will burn,' he said hoarsely, his eyes hooded.

Rosa reached a hand behind her head and pulled her hair-band free, shaking her head to enable her hair to tumble over her shoulders. 'In that case I suggest we go inside. I forfeit the game.'

Nico did not think he had ever been so aroused—not even when he had first seen a picture of a naked woman at the grand old age of nineteen.

This...

How could he ever have thought she was merely pretty? She was beautiful. And how could he ever have thought implanted breasts on 'stick-insects'—as Rosa so eloquently referred to his previous lovers—were attractive? Compared to the creamy, inviting wonder of Rosa's voluptuous figure... there *was* no comparison.

Slowly, he extended a hand. 'If you are forfeiting then I win by default. It is time for me to claim my prize.'

Rosa's chest rose and fell, and the beautiful caramel swirls of her eyes pulled him to her. With only the slightest hint of hesitation she threaded her fingers through his, allowing him to steer her, keeping their fingers laced together.

Nico locked the patio doors behind them before turning to face her.

She stood at the foot of the bed, watching him. It was as if a hook caught in his chest when he caught a glimmer of apprehension in her eyes, confirming his suspicions that she was not quite as blasé as she was trying to portray.

Ridiculously, this touched him.

His usual sleek lovers oozed sexual confidence, knew they looked fantastic clothed or undressed.

Not one of them could hold a torch to Rosa.

A bottle of massage oil had been left on the dressing table, as he had instructed.

'You were confident,' she observed, uttering her first words since she had forfeited.

'I always play to win.'

He stepped over until he stood before her. Unable to resist, he snaked a hand around her neck and gathered that thick mass of hair, inhaling the sweet fragrance. He felt her tremble, heard her breath quicken.

Heat licked through him, as deep a burn as he could stand. He released his hold on her and took a step back, unable to tear his eyes away. 'It is traditional for a massage to be given naked.'

The caramel darkened to chocolate. Keeping her eyes fixed on his, she moved her hands behind her back and unhooked the top of her bikini, then slid the straps down past her shoulders and let it drop to the floor.

For an age all he could do was gaze at her, completely transfixed. Those magnificent breasts he had been dreaming about were more perfect than in his deepest imaginings.

Rosa was all woman—a glorious, hourglass gift from the heavens.

He sensed her arousal. He could see it in the puckering of the perfect pale rose nipples, hear it in the shallowness of her breath, feel it in the heat emanating from her curvy form.

Her fingers tugged at the bikini bottoms.

'No,' he said hoarsely. 'Keep those on.' He did not think he could trust himself if she were to reveal the core of her womanhood to him. Not yet. Not until he had regained some control.

Closing his eyes, he took deep breaths. 'I need you to lie on your stomach.'

When she was lying flat on her belly, her head resting on a pillow, he removed a condom from his wallet and threw it onto the bed before divesting himself of the restrictive shorts. Shamelessly naked, he climbed onto the bed and knelt beside her.

Her ebony hair was spread around her shoulders. With tender care, he gathered it together and swept it down the side of her neck, tucking it under her chin. Her eyes were closed.

She jolted when the first drops of oil hit her back but made no sound.

At first he worked on her neck and the top of her shoulders, determined to release the tension that had been dogging her since their arrival on Butterfly Island, slowly working his way downwards across the sweep of her back. He could not help but marvel at the dewy softness of her skin, his fingers kneading into buttery flesh so reminiscent of a Botticelli painting.

How could he ever have thought lean stick-insects were desirable?

Gradually he reached the top of her rounded buttocks.

So far she had made not the slightest sound. Nothing. Surely she could not have fallen asleep?

That question was answered a moment later when he tugged down on her bikini bottoms and she raised her bottom in the air to assist him.

Nico had to stop what he was doing and check himself. The ache in his loins was no mere pain. It was torture. Pure torture.

Only when he was certain he had control did he slide the bikini bottoms down her smooth, shapely legs and throw them onto the floor. He pressed a kiss to the small of her back and had to check himself again when a tiny whimper escaped from her throat.

Spreading her legs, he knelt between them and rained kisses all over her back, simultaneously massaging her buttocks, her thighs, her waist, touching every part of her, then returning to knead that glorious bottom.

When his lips reached the base of her neck he traced a finger down the cleft between her buttocks, gratified beyond measure when she raised them again for him. Gently he inserted a finger into her velvet warmth and groaned aloud as he was welcomed into her hot moistness.

Another whimper escaped from her throat.

He clamped a hand on her shoulder and finally turned her over.

The sight that greeted him would be forever etched into his memories.

Rosa's cheeks were flushed, her eyes dilated. Her plump lips were a screaming invitation to be kissed...

Nico did not need a second invitation.

Stroking the stray strands of hair off her face, he took possession of the soft plumpness.

The first press of his lips to hers scorched him. If it were possible to combust with a kiss, this was the closest any human had come. The fire that burned through him was almost too much to bear, and when he snaked his tongue into the sweetness of her parted lips he almost pulled away, the intensity too much for any mere mortal to handle...

But then one of Rosa's arms wound around his neck.

Her hand palmed the base of his skull, her fingers scraping through the bristles of his hair, forcing him closer, deepening the kiss, driving away all errant thoughts. He was helpless to do anything but succumb.

He kissed her like a drowning man reaching air, and she responded with the same greedy, furious need, their tongues clashing in a rhythmic duel in which they would both be winners.

Kissing had always been a sop. He had never seen the need for it other than as a means to a greater end.

But he could kiss Rosa for ever—could plunder her mouth with his tongue and lips for eternity. She tasted like nectar.

Her response blew his mind. Her kisses, her touch, all turning the raging burn in his veins into thick lava. She shifted and writhed beneath him, parting her legs, hooking an ankle around his thigh in wordless invitation.

'Not yet,' he murmured into her mouth, before breaking away and trailing kisses down the delicate arch of her neck, further down, until he caught a pink puckered nipple in his mouth.

Her helpless moan fired his fervour. Her small hands cradled his scalp, her back arching in response.

Rosa's breasts were perfection in themselves. Soft and plump and gloriously ripe. He kissed and caressed and sucked and moulded, his free hand trailing down to the mound between her legs, splaying his fingers through damp, downy hair.

He had never been so turned on in his life.

Why, he wondered dimly as he smothered the other glorious nipple with his mouth, did so many women feel the need to display the core of their femininity and turn it into an exhibition? Not Rosa. All of Rosa's secrets were hidden, waiting to be discovered.

'Nico, please—I need you inside me.'

Her husky voice was little more than a whimper. And he needed to be inside her too. Forget the long, languorous bout of lovemaking he had envisaged for them. This was too much. He needed her now.

'Condom.' That was the only word he could manage. A

raging fire was consuming every part of him. He stretched out an arm and snatched the foil wrapper.

Unwilling to break physical contact, still resting between her thighs, he shifted onto his hip. While he ripped the foil with his teeth and unrolled the condom onto an erection that had ever ached more, Rosa wound her arms around his neck and rained kisses down his throat and across his collarbone, her soft lips burning his skin, her teeth nipping at his flesh.

Much more of this and he really would combust.

The condom securely on, Nico wrapped his arms around her tiny waist and pushed her back onto the pillow, possessing her mouth as he positioned himself above the welcoming folds between her legs.

She raised her hips and in one fluid movement he plunged deep into her tight warmth.

Dear sweet heaven…

His eyes flew open to find Rosa's fixed on him, on her face an expression of heavenly wonder.

He wanted to savour it, to relish the sheer, unadulterated pleasure of the moment. But he could not. He kissed her—a brutal clash of lips and teeth and tongue—and began to move, thrusting as deep inside her as he could go.

She moaned deeply, her fingers clasping his buttocks, driving him deeper and deeper, forcing the pace, demanding more, taking every inch of him until he feared he could hold on no further.

Her breaths were becoming shallow, her soft moans becoming longer.

Pulsations were starting to build inside him.

He screwed his eyes shut, fighting with all his might to hold on. This was too soon. Far too soon. He didn't want it to end. He wanted to drive into her tight warmth for ever.

And then her back arched, her muscles spasmed around him and he could hold on no more. With one last bucking thrust he let go and allowed the pulsations to rip through him in a burst of unprecedented exquisite pleasure.

Rosa could not help the laugh that escaped from her throat.

Nico lifted his face from its burial in her shoulder and gazed at her.

'Amazing...' She sighed. Stars were still blinding the back of her retinas. 'Bloody amazing.'

He kissed her—a full-bodied, sensual kiss that contained so much—before breaking away from her.

'I need to get rid of the condom,' he said regretfully, his voice hoarse.

'One more kiss,' she beseeched, yanking his head back down so they could exchange a kiss that was filled more with laughter than passion.

He pressed his lips to the tip of her nose. 'I'll be back in less than a minute.'

'I'll be counting.'

Stretching luxuriantly, she watched him pad over to the *en suite* bathroom.

It was cold without his warmth, so she nestled under the sheets to wait for his return.

She felt ridiculously like giggling.

So *that* was what an orgasm felt like.

This time she did giggle, smothering the schoolgirl sound with a pillow.

Who would have known? How could she ever have known making love to her husband would be so wonderful?

'What's so funny?' Nico came back into the room, stalking towards her, his brow raised and a quirk playing on his lips.

She shook her head. 'Nothing. I was just thinking.'

He got under the covers next to her. 'Thinking about what?'

'Thinking I can't believe we shared a roof for eleven

months and had no idea how incredible things could be between us.'

A pang of anxiety suddenly bloomed through her.

'It wasn't just me, was it?' she begged, turning onto her
side to face him and sliding her hand around his waist. 'Tell
me it was as good for you.'

He pulled her close so she was flush against him and
breathed into her hair. 'How can you even question it?'

Her mind at ease, she buried her face into his chest, inhaling the citrusy scent that now contained a hint of musk.

Had she ever felt so...replete? Content? Whatever the
word, all she knew was right at that moment it would take a
crowbar to prise her away from him.

Nico had taken her to the stars and she never wanted to
come back to earth.

CHAPTER TEN

'WAKE UP, SLEEPY HEAD.'

Nico's gravelly voice broke through Rosa's slumber. Instantly her brain switched to wakefulness.

As with the day before, he had brought her breakfast in bed.

Stretching, she covered a yawn and sat up.

What a difference a day made.

Twenty-four hours ago she had woken stiff and shattered. Today she felt as if she had slept for England. Not that she'd had that much sleep, considering they had still been making love when the sun began its ascent.

'What game are you planning to teach me today?' she asked, picking up the glass of orange juice.

A wicked gleam came into Nico's eyes. 'Today, *daragaya*, you and I are going on a trip.'

'Where to? The gym?' She guffawed at her own joke. Unbelievably, she was already wide awake, her entire being fizzing with delight, her heart so full she could believe it had been filled with a forest of rose petals.

He leaned down and grazed his teeth along the curve of her neck. 'Eat your breakfast and then change into one of those tiny bikinis that show off your beautiful body.'

'You want me to change?' she said, turning the sides of

her mouth down and fluttering her eyelashes at him. 'That's a shame. I was hoping we could spend the rest of the day in bed.'

Capturing her mouth in a kiss, he nipped her bottom lip gently. 'Nothing would please me more than to spend the rest of the week in bed with you, but as this is your first holiday I want you to remember it for more than fantastic sex.'

With hungry eyes she watched him retreat into the *en suite* bathroom and released a sigh of contentment.

Impulsively she pinched her forearm.

It hurt.

She threw herself back and gazed at the ceiling, a smile glued to her face.

This really was real.

For the first time since she was eight years old she wanted to hug herself with happiness.

An hour later they stood with the Captain on the main deck. The back of the yacht had been rolled open. Ahead of them, rising from the ocean like the kind of deserted island found in all good films, sat uninhabited King Island.

'You expect me to get on that?' she asked, pointing at the jet ski that had been brought out. The Captain had assured them that snorkelling gear and a picnic had been placed in its inbuilt storage box.

'That's how we're getting to the island,' Nico said, throwing her a life jacket. 'Now, put that on.'

She looked at the fluorescent material with doubt and not a little fear. 'Won't the orange clash with my sunburn?'

He simply stared at her, arms folded, brows raised.

'I don't see why we can't sail to the island like normal people,' she grumbled.

'Where would the fun be in that?' A gorgeous smile broke out on his poker-straight face. 'We're on holiday. Let's make the most of it.'

She stared uncertainly at the jet ski. To her eyes it was a huge, fat, two-seater motorbike with the wheels missing.

'I'll be driving it,' he said, clearly reading her mind. 'You will be perfectly safe. You just have to hold on tight to me.'

Despite herself, those now familiar bubbles of excitement started causing a riot in her belly. In her heart she knew Nico would never do anything that would put her in harm's reach. When she had given herself to him she had given more than just her body and her heart. She had given him her trust.

Before she could act, Nico closed the gap between them, pulled the life jacket from her hands and manhandled her arms into it. 'That's better,' he said, a smirk playing on his lips as he zipped it up securely.

She glared at him. 'I am perfectly capable of putting a life jacket on myself, thank you.'

'If you'd dithered any longer the sun would have been setting.'

Despite herself, she laughed, shaking her head at his high-handed arrogance—an arrogance tempered by the amusement in his eyes.

Naturally he eschewed her demands that he too wear a life jacket, jumping onto the machine dressed only in a pair of long navy swimming shorts.

Holding on to the handlebars, he flashed his white teeth. 'Well? Are you getting on? Or do you want me to carry you on?'

'You wouldn't dare,' she said, knowing perfectly well that he would dare. He wouldn't think twice about it.

Not giving him the chance, she climbed on behind him, wrapped her arms around his waist and they were off.

Her head pressed into his back, she clung to him. Over the ocean they flew, cutting through bobbing waves, the speed making her hair splay in all directions, the spray of salt water tempering the blazing heat of the sun on her semi-naked form.

All too soon they came to a stop on a smooth white beach.

'That was fantastic!' she exclaimed with a beam of delight.

Nico grinned and took her hand to steady her wobbly legs as she climbed off. 'Exhilarating, isn't it?'

'Can we do it again for longer?'

He mock-bowed. 'Your wish is my command. But let us explore the island and eat first.'

King Island was much smaller than Butterfly Island, and much less verdant, but it contained the same tropical feel. If a castaway should appear with a parrot on his shoulder she wouldn't bat an eyelash. As far as Rosa was concerned, it was perfect.

Hands clasped together, they traversed the beach, paddling through the shallow water before finding a small cove that was perfect for their picnic, away from any prying eyes on the yacht.

Nico unpacked their feast of goodies. For a while they ate in companionable silence. The sun beamed down, and the fresh scent of shrubbery and exotic flowers filled Rosa's senses with such warmth and contentment she feared she could explode from the joy of it all.

Was this how normal people felt? What normal people experienced? The heady rush of falling in love, of embracing the pleasures life had to offer instead of hiding away in a self-built fortress?

'How long after the contracts are signed will you start building here?' she asked, referring to the accommodation and facilities that were to be built there for the offshore workers.

'Within weeks.'

She sighed sadly.

'What's the matter?'

'It seems a shame to spoil all this beauty.'

He reached out a hand and tilted her chin. 'You have seen

the plans. Robert and I agreed the only development done here would be sympathetic to the landscape. I promise you I will keep to my word.'

'I know.' She smiled. Impulsively, she darted up and pressed a kiss to his lips. 'You're a good man, Nicolai Baranski.'

For a moment darkness clouded his eyes, before he blinked it away and flashed a mocking grin. 'Don't tell anyone else that.'

She looked at him carefully, looking for a clue as to what could have caused that brief cloud. Apart from a gleam in his eye there was nothing to be found.

She shoved the image away to be pondered another time. Right then everything was perfect, and she didn't want anything to intrude and mar it.

She wrapped her arms around his neck. 'I wouldn't dream of telling anyone. After all, we have your reputation to protect.'

Hooking an arm around her waist, he lowered her onto her back and nuzzled her neck. 'Speaking of protecting reputations, you *do* realise it has been a whole four hours since this bad Russian playboy has made love to his beautiful English wife?'

'Then I suggest we do something about it,' she said, her words coming out in tiny gasps as she felt his erection press against her thigh.

Her gasps soon turned into soft mews when Nico divested her of her bikini and got down to some serious reputation-salvaging...

After a day spent exploring King Island and each other, and a mammoth, exhilarating ride on the jet ski, they'd returned to the yacht for dinner, which they'd eaten on the sundeck.

Now they were both sprawled on the bed, as naked as the

day they had been born, watching *Dr Zhivago* on a cinema screen which was connected to the internet.

'How many times have you watched this?' Nico asked, carefully placing a trail of cherries along her spine.

She shrugged and pressed a foot against his leg. 'No idea.'

He tapped her bottom. 'Don't move.'

She cocked her head back and speared him with a look. 'You're distracting me.'

'That was my intention.'

Her eyes gleamed. 'Carry on.'

Carry on? He could make love to her all night.

Luckily they still had another four days together. That would be plenty of time to get this mass of unprecedented desire out of his system. Life could then return to normal, with the added bonus of sharing his beautiful wife's body every night when he was in the UK. Unless, of course, he could convince her to take a permanent role as his PA.

One by one he ate the cherries off her back, then got down to some proper distraction business.

Even the moon had disappeared by the time they were finally spent and he turned the light off.

Sleepily, she prodded him with her foot. 'Keep it on.'

'Right. Sorry.' He fiddled with the switches until he found the bathroom light and turned it on, filling the cabin with a dim, warm glow. Curiosity finally got the better of him. 'If you're not afraid of the dark, why do you like to have the light on?'

'I can see if anyone sneaks into the room.'

Thinking she had made a joke, Nico started to laugh, but then he remembered all the times he had passed her room at night and seen a dim glow seeping from under her doorframe. He had always assumed she was reading or watching television. How many times had he fought his yen to open the door...?

He blinked the thought away.

'Do I take it someone once came into your room in the dark and scared you?'

She yawned and snuggled into him. 'Nico, it's late and I'm shattered. Can we have this conversation in the morning?'

'No.' He should be shattered too. Physically, he was. But his brain was still fully wired. 'You always shy away from discussing your past or anything personal.' So did he. Normally. But right then he did not feel normal. Not by a long chalk.

'That's the way we always liked it.'

'If someone has hurt or scared you it is my business to know.' And when he learned *who* had hurt and scared Rosa he would track that person down and give them the fright of their life. No one hurt his wife. *No one.*

'It was a long time ago. All children are hurt and scared at some point.'

He forced his voice to stay even, trying to control the wild flurry of his thoughts. 'What happened?'

'Nothing *happened*,' she said quietly. 'There were a couple of bullies in one of the children's homes I lived in for a while. They thought it was funny to sneak into the younger kids' rooms and scare us.' She raised her head and rested her chin on his chest. 'One particularly well-executed torment was to hide under our beds and then, after the lights had been turned out, to grab our legs. In my case, the monster under the bed was two fourteen-year-old girls.'

The hairs on his arms rose. Everything she had said made his skin crawl, but out of everything one pertinent fact leapt out at him. 'You lived in a children's home?'

'Yes.'

His voice became hoarse. 'When? Why?'

She was silent for a few moments, as if weighing up

whether or not to confide in him. 'My mother abandoned me to Social Services when I was five.'

Blood rushed to his brain, the pressure inside his head pounding with the weight of a dozen hammers. 'Your mother *abandoned* you?'

It took guts for him to keep you. He must love you very much. Her words echoed around his head. Why hadn't he paid attention to the wistful tone in which those words had been delivered?

'I thought you were an orphan.' He raked a hand through his hair as he distinctly recalled her stating when they'd married that her parents were both dead. He had never questioned her on this—had assumed she had been an adult when they'd died.

'My dad died when I was a baby,' she said, and the light in her voice that had been so prevalent throughout the day had diminished into a dispassionate tone he recognised but could not place. 'My mum died a couple of years ago.'

'Did you go back to live with her?' he asked hopefully. The thought of Rosa living in the care system tore at something inside of him.

'No. She never came back for me.'

Silence rent the cabin, the proportions of which seemed to have shrunk into a tiny bubble. The only movement was his fingers, running through her hair like a comb.

He knew he should leave it there. They had made love. That did not mean he had to know her innermost secrets. He did not know what had compelled him to question her in the first place.

'Tell me,' he commanded in a voice that was not quite steady.

Her chest lifted as she expelled a long sigh. 'There isn't much to tell. My parents were really young when they had me—only sixteen. Dad was a bit of a hothead, by all accounts, and died in a motorbike accident. Then her own mother died and my mum couldn't cope raising me on her own.'

He swallowed. 'They told you this?'

Her head moved, her thick hair tickling his chin. 'I was allowed to see my file when I turned eighteen.' A touch of sadness crept into her voice. 'I always thought—hoped—I was dumped because she couldn't afford to keep me. I thought the social worker was protecting me from something terrible, like drug abuse or...or something. But money and drugs didn't have anything to do with it. She just didn't want me back. Social Services held out for three years in the hope she would take me back before approving me as a candidate for adoption.'

Nico swore under his breath.

'Unfortunately eight-year-olds aren't at the top of any potential adopters' wish-lists.'

He closed his eyes at the matter-of-fact, fatalistic tone to her voice and wrapped his arms around her, as if the very act could protect her and keep her safe. How could anyone treat a child in such a manner?

And what kind of a monster was he, to live with someone, to forge a life with them—yes, an unconventional life, but a life all the same—and not know something so fundamental about her?

'Could your mother have been suffering from depression?' he suggested, his brain scrambling to think of something that would explain such heartless behaviour. 'She had lost your father and her own mother in a short space of time.'

'I tracked her down five years ago.'

There was that catch in her throat again—a catch that leapt out and jumped right into his heart.

'She was embarrassed to see me. I think it shamed her, having me on her doorstep, reminding her of a life she had tried to forget. She'd remarried and had another child. A boy.

A brother I never knew existed. She was polite, but...' Her voice was fading, becoming little more than a whisper. 'She didn't want me there. It was obvious. I gave her my details but I never heard from her again.'

'I'm sorry.' His words sounded ridiculous to his own ears. How could a mere *sorry* compensate for a lifetime of abandonment?

'What for?' Surprise laced her husky voice.

'I never knew.'

'It's not something I shout about.' She disentangled herself from his tight hold and rolled onto her back. He could see her profile, her snub nose pointing upwards as she gazed at the ceiling. 'Us care-home kids have a bad rep. Most people think kids in care are drug-addicted no-hopers. We're expected to fail. And for the most part we do.'

'*You* didn't fail,' he said, outraged on her behalf.

'I was lucky. I had a social worker who believed in me, and at one point I was placed with a foster family who were fanatical about the need for a good education. It was through them that I learned I had a good brain and a talent for languages—Dacha, the foster mum, was Russian.'

'Did she teach you the language?'

'Only a few words and phrases—I only stayed with them for a year—but I learned to love the sound of it. Russian is a beautiful language.'

'Why did you only stay with them for a year?'

'They had a baby of their own so I had to move out.'

'What? Because they had a baby?'

'The baby needed a nursery. I had the only spare room.'

There was that dispassionate tone again—the tone that sliced through his skin and into his core. 'Stupid me thought they were going to adopt me.' She sighed deeply, then rolled onto her side again and snuggled back into him. 'Can we stop talking about this now? I'm tired and I need to get some sleep.'

Nico knew he should heed her request and drop the subject. Rosa's past was none of his business. He had got what he wanted. He had proved they were compatible in bed—hell, *compatible* was an understatement. Together they were spectacular.

Now she belonged to him and no one else. He could share her brain, her wit and her body. Everything else was superfluous.

And yet...

'What about your brother?' he asked. He couldn't let the matter drop. The need to find some light for her was becoming of the utmost importance. *Please*, let there be some light. 'Have you met him? How old is he?'

'He's twenty.' Quickly Nico did the maths. Rosa's brother had been born just two years after she had been abandoned. 'He called to let me know our mother had died—he'd found the letter I gave her with my contact details on it.'

'That was good of him.'

'He called *after* the funeral. Out of courtesy. I've only had contact with him once since. Now, can I please go to sleep?'

Nico's hands balled into fists even as he kissed the top of her head and wished her a reluctant goodnight.

There was still so much he wanted to know.

How did a child go through what she had been through and grow up to be such a *good* person? There was nothing in Rosa's personality to hint at her traumatic childhood and adolescence.

Or was there?

Maybe the clues were there if you searched hard enough.

She was personable. Everyone liked her. But could anyone say they *knew* her? Really knew her? He suspected the answer to that was no. Rosa did not have a single close friend.

No wonder she had jumped at the idea of marrying him. She had been effectively alone since early childhood—and what was it she had said to him when they were scribbling their marriage contract? *'This will suit me perfectly. I've always liked the idea of being part of a couple—well, being part of a unit—but...'* There she had shrugged, her nose wrinkling. *'The rest of it...no, thank you. My head is private.'*

Nico had thought he understood what she could not articulate. They were two of a kind. Emotional intimacy repulsed them both.

Now he wondered if it really did repulse her, or if it were just a barrier she had erected to protect herself.

What had changed? Why did she want to leave a marriage that gave her everything she needed without having to put up with the nonsense she didn't want?

The answer became obvious.

Rosa wanted more. She had said so herself the day she'd asked for a divorce. He had simply misinterpreted it.

He had spent two days and nights making love to her, blithely unaware of the emotional damage she had sustained.

His stupid pride had been so injured when she'd had the temerity to sleep with another man, that not once had he properly considered *why* she had ricocheted back into her ex-boyfriend's arms. He had assumed her loneliness was of a sexual kind.

A roll of nausea swelled in his stomach, beads of perspiration breaking out on his forehead.

He pulled her closer. She felt so good in his arms. Better than he could ever have imagined.

But Rosa needed something he could never give her. She needed someone to love her.

If they'd had this conversation before—even two days ago—he would never have made love to her.

He had married her believing she had the same emotional deficiency as himself.

He could not have got it more wrong if he had tried.

He expelled a shuddering breath.

'Are you okay?' she said into his chest, her voice thick with sleep.

'Everything is fine.' He traced his fingers lightly across her back. 'Get some sleep.'

That was the first lie he had ever told her. Everything was *not* fine.

Nico was incapable of returning love. He was incapable of reciprocating emotion. This deficiency on his part had already caused one woman real pain. He would not allow it to damage Rosa too. She deserved—hell, she *needed*—so much more than he could ever give.

What he needed was to end this. He needed to end this now. Before she gave her heart to him. Before he caused her any more damage.

CHAPTER ELEVEN

Rosa lay like a starfish in the swimming pool, letting the morning heat be absorbed into her skin. A smile played on her lips—the same smile she had woken with, even though she had been alone in the bed. Nico must have gone for his morning exercise, which had put paid to her idea of surprising him with breakfast in bed.

It would have been wonderful to do something nice for him. Whatever his motivations, there was no denying that he had gone out of his way to ensure that this, their first holiday together—and her first holiday ever—was as relaxing as it could possibly be. All she wanted was to make a gesture to show how much she appreciated everything he had done.

It was hard to credit that she had married him believing herself to be safe. Marrying a control freak like Nico—a man she had believed incapable of affection or empathy—had seemed ideal for what she had needed. Looking back, she was glad she hadn't known how her feelings towards him would change. If she'd had a crystal ball she never would have married him.

Thank God she didn't have a crystal ball.

Under that tough, controlling exterior lay a loyal and thoughtful man and a thrillingly tender lover. And he cared. He really cared.

She could no more have stopped herself from falling in

love with him than she could have stopped the blazing sun from rising.

When he had still not appeared after she had spent thirty minutes lazing in the pool, she ordered breakfast for herself. She was halfway through a bacon sandwich when he appeared from the stairs on the second deck, wearing only a pair of gym shorts with a towel slung round his neck.

'Morning.' She beamed, rising from her chair in anticipation of his kiss.

Nico nodded briefly and looked at his watch. 'Good morning. Did you sleep well?'

'Wonderfully, thank you. How did you sleep?'

'Fine.' He looked at his watch again.

'You snuck out of bed early. Was I snoring?'

Only the briefest glimmer of a smile curved his lips, but he still did not look at her. 'Not at all.'

She swallowed a throat that had suddenly and inexplicably gone dry. 'Have you eaten?'

'Yes. I need to shower. Finish your breakfast. I'll join you in a while.'

Her heart thundering painfully against her ribs, she watched him disappear into their suite.

He closed the patio door behind him.

Dimly aware she was still standing, she sat back down.

Nico had not looked her in the eyes once during that short exchange.

Her stomach rolled. She gazed at the bacon sandwich still in her hand and placed it back on the plate. Her appetite, which mere moments ago had been ravenous, had deserted her.

If she had not lived with Nico for nearly a year she would have shrugged off his strange mood, putting it down to him not being a morning person. Plenty of people weren't—herself included.

Nico was not one of them. Nico awoke early every morning, firing on all cylinders. Especially after his morning workout.

She didn't realise she had nibbled her little fingernail down too far until he returned a good half-hour later. By then her breakfast had been cleared away and a fresh pot of coffee brought to the sundeck.

'I did debate ordering us a cocktail each,' she said as he took the seat opposite. 'But I thought you would only complain it didn't match your standards.' Deliberately she kept her tone light, hoping the unease rippling through her was nothing but the workings of a paranoid mind. Her paranoia had been fed a little more by the polo shirt he wore, which covered his chest.

'Very wise.' The tiniest ghost of smile played on his lips. His eyes were unreadable.

'So, what do you fancy doing today?' she asked, chattering madly to fill the tense silence that had appeared between them. 'As we're in the middle of the open ocean I'm guessing another trip to a deserted island is out of the question. Are there many other board games you can teach me? I'd love to learn backgammon...'

'Rosa, we need to talk.'

Her mouth shut with a snap.

He poured them both a coffee and slid her cup to her. 'The divorce you want...I am in agreement.'

Her lips parted, forming a perfect O. But nothing came out. If she'd had sails he would have literally knocked the wind out of them.

Nico rested his elbows on the table and took a sip of his coffee. Finally he looked at her. 'I don't want you to get the wrong idea—the past couple of days have been great—but in hindsight I think our becoming lovers was a mistake.'

Frozen, she continued to gaze at him, unable to blink.

There was nothing to read on his face. It held the same dispassionate expression it had contained when she had told him she wanted a divorce.

'I misunderstood what you meant when you said you wanted more from a marriage,' he continued. 'I took it to mean you wanted sex to be a part of it. I did not realise you were looking for something deeper. If I had known of your history I would never have allowed us to sleep together.'

Deep inside her belly all the lovely, warm, mushy feelings that had been swirling there since they had first made love solidified into compacted ice. Her blood thickened into slush; her head was a pounding torment of hammers.

Forcing deep breaths into her lungs, she counted to ten before dredging up a smile. 'I really don't know where you got the idea I wanted something deeper, Nico,' she said. Thank God her vocal cords were working properly. 'I said I wanted something more than what we had. I never actually said *what* I wanted, or said I wanted it with *you.*' It gave her enormous, bitter satisfaction to witness disconcertion flittering across his features. 'But you are right in one respect—the last couple of days *have* been great. I really feel as if I've had a proper holiday, so thank you for that. I'll be sure to include regular breaks in my schedule. And you're excellent in bed. Congratulations.'

Nico blanched—whether at her saccharinely sweet delivered words or the *faux* sincere manner in which she was delivering them, she couldn't have cared less.

'And congratulations for managing the equivalent of three days with me,' she continued. 'Is that a record for you? But, *purlease*, it *was* only sex—and, as great as it was, I have no interest in pursuing a deeper relationship with a man who has the emotional maturity of a walnut.'

His eyes glittered, a deep crease furrowing in his brow. 'Rosa, I never—'

'A word of advice,' she interrupted, getting to her feet. 'When you're standing in a deep hole, stop digging.'

'Where are you going?' he asked as she walked off towards the cabin.

'To get some suncream,' she called back over her shoulder. 'It looks like today is going to be another scorcher and I don't fancy burning—I'd hate to clash with the life jacket should the yacht capsize.'

When she had disappeared from view Nico took a deep breath and closed his eyes.

That had been harder than he'd expected. Much harder. Through his extended workout he had been mulling over the best choice of words to use. He had known he could not put it off, but for once there had been inertia in his body's response. For once the thought of ending a relationship had caused his stomach to cramp.

He hadn't lied. They truly had been great together. The past three days had been the best of his life. If ever there was a woman he *could* love, Rosa would be the one.

But he did not know how to love. He did not know how to give a woman what she needed. And the last thing he wanted was to hurt the one woman in the world he liked and respected.

It had hurt his heart to look at her.

When he had said what needed to be said he had forced his eyes to stay locked on her, forced himself to witness the shock she had not been quick enough to hide.

Her shock had not lasted long. He should have known she would not react in the way he'd anticipated. Not for Rosa the tantrums and sulks he had become accustomed to. Apart from her initial shock, she couldn't have cared less.

Had he really read her so wrong?

Had her childhood hardened her so much that she was incapable of loving too?

The thought should dispel some of his nagging guilt. It did not.

Rosa's shock had been real. That tiny tic of hers, although barely perceptible, had been revealing.

It was not long before she came back out to the sundeck in a black bikini, white shorts and dark sunglasses. She marched over to him.

'Could you put some suncream on my back, please?' She thrust the bottle into the hand he automatically stretched out. Not waiting for an answer, she turned her back to him and lifted her ponytail.

He had no good reason to refuse.

'Are we going to return to Butterfly Island before schedule?' she asked whilst he poured the thick cream onto the palm of a hand.

'I will speak to the Captain shortly.' Using brisk motions he slathered the cream onto her back, wishing his fingers didn't delight in the buttery skin. He counted four moles and compressed his lips tightly together. His skin tingled. He was filled with the need to slip a hand round and cup one of those full...

'Good. It is pointless continuing with this cruise when there is work we can be getting on with. Are you done?'

He blinked and quickly moved his hands away. 'Yes.' He clenched them into fists lest he gave in to the urge to slap her perfectly rounded bottom.

'Thank you.' She flashed him a quick smile and padded over to the pool.

Nico supressed a groan as she casually stripped off the shorts and placed them neatly on a lounger. She then unfolded a towel, spread it out on the adjacent lounger, and settled down under the blazing sun.

He must be mad, he reflected, gritting his teeth at the ache rampaging through his loins. If he had kept his mouth shut for a couple more days he could be down there, lazing by the pool, with the most responsive, intuitive woman he had ever been blessed to make love with.

Until today he had never ended a relationship before it had run its course. Admittedly, it didn't take long for him to become bored with a lover, but Rosa was different. He had never had a lover like Rosa before.

He dragged his fingers through his hair and got to his feet. It was time to tell the Captain they needed to change course and return to Butterfly Island.

With a pang of dread he acknowledged they would have to spend at least one more night together.

Her eyes hidden behind the thick sunglasses, Rosa watched Nico leave the sundeck.

She wanted to throw up. If it were not for her pride she would be holed up in the bathroom at that very minute.

At least she had managed to salvage some dignity from the situation. But then, having spent her life coping with rejection, she had become an expert at handling it.

This time would be no different.

Nico spent the rest of the day with the crew. The Captain had agreed to increase the speed they were sailing at. With any luck they should return to shore tomorrow evening. The Captain had also agreed to show him how the yacht was run, and he had thoroughly enjoyed exploring the bowels of the ship and learning of the mechanics behind it.

The sun had long set and thick clouds were encroaching over the sky when his thoughts turned to Rosa. All day her image had flickered at the back of his retinas, but he had refused to allow her space in his head. Thinking of her made his chest tighten too strongly for comfort.

He hoped she had remembered to eat. She had a habit of skipping meals when she was bogged down with work.

Then he remembered she had nothing to distract her from eating.

He found her sitting cross-legged under the covers of the enormous bed, working on a laptop set upon her knees. No doubt she had taken sanctuary indoors because of the brewing storm.

She lifted her head briefly and nodded at him.

'You're wearing glasses,' he said, blinking with surprise at the pink-rimmed frames.

'Well spotted.' Her focus went back to whatever she was doing.

'I didn't know you wore glasses.' How was that even possible?

'I have continuous-wear contact lenses, but the ones I had with me were nearing the end of their shelf-life. If I had known I would be away for longer than a day I would have made sure I brought my supplies with me.' She threw him an accusatory glare. 'Luckily I keep a spare pair of glasses in my handbag.'

He surveyed her warily. Rosa's frame was taut, as if she were contracting all her muscles. 'They suit you.'

Her lips tightened into a white line and she tapped furiously at the keys in front of her. 'Whatever.'

He raised a brow at the inflection of her tone. 'They *do* suit you.'

'Nicolai, I am perfectly aware glasses make me look like a troll. Please don't try to be nice to me.'

'I'm not trying to be nice.' He ran a hand through his hair and shook his head. For someone who professed to be cool about the turn their relationship had taken, she was acting extremely strangely. 'I don't know where you got the idea you look like a troll...'

'From the mirror—all right?' she snapped, slamming the lid of the laptop down and staring at him with a look of untamed wildness behind the clear lenses. Her eyes were strangely magnified. 'Believe me, I am well aware of how I look—of the ugly, vertically challenged frump who's reflected back at me.'

'You are *not* ugly,' he snapped back, outraged she could even think such a thing.

'I'm hardly the kind of long-legged, blonde-haired beauty you usually cavort with.' She pushed the laptop off her lap and slithered out from under the covers.

Nico had no idea what he could say to that last remark without making matters worse. For all her tightly controlled exterior something was clearly eating at her, and for once he didn't have a clue how to approach her.

She jumped off the bed, her braless breasts bouncing softly under a thin white vest. The only other item of clothing she wore was a pair of skimpy lace knickers. Knickers *he* had instructed be included in her wardrobe when seduction had been at the forefront of his mind.

At this stage seduction should be the last thing on his mind, but watching her stride forcefully across the cabin floor, he felt that familiar ache well inside him. If he was being honest with himself the ache hadn't really left him, had been a constant reminder of how mind-blowing things had been between them.

'Where did you get the laptop from?' he asked, coughing to clear the lump that had formed in his throat. He needed to get away from personal territory. He had opened a big enough can of worms the day before, by pumping her for information that should have been left alone.

'Patrick lent it to me,' she said, referring to one of the

crew members. She stepped into her dressing room, leaving the door open. He watched as she rummaged through some drawers.

'What were you working on?'

'It's personal.' She bent over to step into the yellow skirt she had selected. Anyone else and he would suspect her of being deliberately provocative. Instead he could feel the taut anger reverberating through her, pulsing through the physical distance she had placed between them and hitting him with the force of a Taser.

He should let it go. Hadn't he learned by now that with Rosa he should leave well enough alone, if only for his own sanity?

His mind flickered back to their last night on Butterfly Island and her suspicious behaviour before they had gone to dinner. 'Is this what you were doing the other night, before we went to dinner with Robert and Laura?'

Why was he even pretending to care?

Deep inside Rosa's bones a fire raged—a fire she had spent the day obstinately refusing to admit even existed. For the first time since she had married Nico the fire had nothing to do with lust or desire. This was rage—a simmering inferno of anger. And now, with him conversing so casually, acting as if nothing had happened—as if he hadn't dumped her and then left her to her own lonely devices for the day—the inferno was approaching boiling point.

She would not allow it to spill over. Whatever happened, she would never let him know the utter devastation he had wrought.

She answered him only when she was certain her tongue could be kept under control. A stupid thing, to think a tongue could take a life of its own, when it was her brain and consciousness that controlled it, but over the past few days it felt as if all the control she had spent years cultivating and perfecting was being ground into dust.

'Yes,' she said, zipping the skirt and smoothing it down. 'It's what I was doing the other night.'

'And are you going to share what you have been doing with *me*?'

'If you must know, I've been trying to trace my father's family.'

He was silent before cautiously asking, 'Are you having any luck?'

'No.'

'What sites have you tried?'

She closed the dressing room door and told him briefly of the ancestry and genealogy sites she had signed up to.

'Have you searched on the social networking sites?'

She threw him a look of disdain and immediately wished she hadn't. Looking at him hurt. 'I've searched everywhere. I've got copies of his birth and death certificates, but the only thing I know for certain is he was an only child. His parents died young. His father was an only child too, but his mother had a sister who emigrated to Australia decades ago. In the year I've been searching she's the only possible surviving relative I've found. I have no idea where in Australia she is, or if she's married or...anything.'

'I know a good private investigator in Australia,' he said. 'If you give me your great-aunt's details I can get him to look into it.'

'No, thank you,' she said stiffly, forcing her legs to walk past him to the stupidly enormous bed. 'I'm happy to take my time. I have no intention of reaching out to her.'

Nico was the last person she wanted help from. All she wanted from him was his signature on the divorce papers.

How dared he lead her on? How dared he say he wanted a proper marriage when all he'd really wanted was to get into her knickers? She had trusted him, and all along he had been pretending, playing a role.

She could hear his brain ticking. She wouldn't put it past him to hire the investigator whether she agreed to it or not.

'What about your mother's family?' he asked quietly.

She carefully picked up the laptop. 'All dead. My mother was the only child of elderly parents—her mother was forty-four when she had her. In those days that really was old to be a mother.' Unwilling to continue the conversation a second longer, she tucked the laptop under her arm. 'I need to get this back to Patrick before he finishes for the evening.'

'I'll come with you,' Nico offered.

'I'm quite capable of walking down two flights of stairs on my own,' she said tersely. She didn't want to be anywhere near him.

In fact, she decided, as she passed through the saloon, she would spend the night in here. The leather sofas were comfortable and it would be easy enough to borrow a blanket. Anything had to be better than sharing a bed with a man for whom two nights with her had most definitely been enough.

CHAPTER TWELVE

Nico found himself checking his watch for the umpteenth time. Rosa should have returned to their suite hours ago.

He would not check on her. Even he had been able to recognise the 'get lost' vibes she had been expelling. Although it went against the grain, he knew he needed to respect her need for space. If he had considered her needs in the first place he would never have got them into this mess.

Leaving her alone for the day had been a bad move on his part. Who could blame her for working all the hours humanly possible when such darkness resided in her head? And why the hell hadn't he left all talk of divorce until they were back on *terra firma*?

But how could he have lived with himself if he had continued to make love to her knowing she believed things between them were something they were not?

Nausea rolled in his stomach with the same motion as the rolling yacht. The incoming storm was proving strong enough to overpower the state-of-the-art stabilisers. He hoped Rosa wasn't outside in it.

Turning onto his side, he stared at her pillow before rolling back and staring at the ceiling. He took another look at his watch.

Screw it. He would never get any sleep until he knew she was all right.

He pulled on a pair of shorts before walking down the steps to the second deck. The saloon was empty. All the rooms on the deck were empty.

The thick storm clouds that had been brewing over them had burst; fat drops of rain were falling like a sheet, the noise almost deafening. His concern was on the verge of turning into something deeper when he spotted her outside. She was leaning on the railings, gazing out into the black nothingness, seemingly oblivious to the wind and rain lashing around her.

His fear should have been allayed by the sight of her. Instead his pulse surged. There was something about the way she stood and her dishevelled appearance that raised his antennae.

He opened the door and stepped out into the storm. 'What are you doing out here?' he asked, forced to raise his voice to be heard over the crashing waves.

She spun around to face him, clutching the tall glass of clear fluid in her hand. 'Nothing.'

'Nothing?' He searched her face, his heart plummeting at the desolation he found there. Deliberately he kept his voice even and non-threatening. 'Please, Rosa, come away from the railing.'

'I'm not in the mood for your company.'

'Have you been drinking?'

'What's it to you?' she said stiffly. 'Now, please leave me alone.'

'Vodka and low railings do not go together—especially in a storm.'

'Why? Are you worried I might fall overboard?' She shook her head and rolled her eyes. 'Please, Nico, don't act as if you care.'

He winced. 'Of course I care.'

Any desolation cleared, her face transforming into an animalistic snarl. The glass in her hand went sailing past him and shattered on the wooden deck. Before he could process what she had just done she roared at him. 'How *dare* you come out here pretending you give a damn about me?'

Stunned at her words and actions, he blinked in astonishment. Nico had barely heard Rosa raise her voice before.

'Well? Are you not going to answer me?' she shouted. 'Or are you too busy thinking of some more good excuses to justify dumping me?'

'I didn't dump you...'

'Don't you dare lie to me!' she screamed, pounding her fists against his chest. 'Don't you bloody dare! I should have known better than to trust you! You're just like everyone else!'

'Rosa, stop it!'

Somehow he managed to gather her wrists together and pull her under the overhang, away from the pouring rain. She struggled. When he refused to relinquish his hold she kicked him in the shins. It would have hurt, but her wet feet were bare.

'Rosa, stop,' he commanded.

Whether it was the authority in his tone or her complete inability to wriggle out of his hold, she stopped struggling and gazed at him. To his horror, her magnified eyes filled and her chin wobbled a fraction.

'Tell me what's wrong with me,' she said, her voice now little more than a whisper. 'Please—just tell me. What is so wrong that no one wants me?'

He shook his head and swore under his breath. 'Rosa, there is nothing wrong with you.'

For a moment she looked as unsure and vulnerable as a child. Relinquishing his hold on her wrists, he reached a hand to her shoulder, but she stiffened at his touch and shrank away, back into the deluge.

The driving rain saturated her, making her appear smaller and more vulnerable than anything he could have conjured in

his darkest nightmares. She seemed oblivious to it. 'All I've
ever wanted was to feel as if I belong somewhere. But there
is nowhere for me. I tried with Stephen. I really, really tried.
But it wasn't there. I wanted to love him but I couldn't, and I
hurt him. I hurt him as badly as my mother hurt me.'

He opened his mouth but she shook her head, her voice
now full of despair.

'Do you know why I got together with him? Call me shallow, but it was because he said I was pretty. No one had ever
called me that before. All my life I've known there's something wrong with me, that I'm ugly...'

'You are not ugly!' Nico could not stomach another word.
Stepping forward, he palmed her cheeks and forced her to
look at him. 'You are *not* ugly. And nor are you pretty. Rosa,
you're *beautiful*—inside and out.'

She swiped him away. 'Then why don't you want me any
more? I've been thinking it over and over and I can't think of
any other reason. I put my trust in you. You said you wanted
a proper marriage and I believed you. You're not a liar, Nico,
so you must have meant it. But the second you got me into
bed and became intimate with me you no longer wanted me.
So please, I beg you, tell me what is wrong with me?'

Nico dragged his hand down his face, breathing deeply to
catch hold of himself.

The pain in her eyes was almost more than he could bear
to witness. All his worst fears were crashing down on him
and it was so much worse than he could have imagined. 'You
are one of the best people I have ever known,' he said, trying
to process his thoughts into some semblance of order. 'You
deserve someone who will love and cherish you, and I wish
to God that someone could be me.'

'But it can't be you, can it? Two nights was enough for you
to realise there is something rotten about me...'

'No!' For the first time in his life he pulled a woman into

his arms for the sole purpose of providing comfort. Wrapping his arms tightly around her so she couldn't wriggle free, he buried his face in her soaking hair and breathed her in. He felt her glasses dislodged against his chest and something inside him cracked.

'Listen to me,' he said, speaking into her hair. 'I *did* want a proper marriage, but my definition of that was for us to continue exactly as we were with sex thrown into the mix. I thought that was what you wanted too. I didn't realise how badly you needed something more. I wish I could be the one to give it to you but I'm not made that way.'

She tried to twist out of his hold but he kept her pressed against him. He could feel the warmth of her breath against his chest and dug his fingers into her scalp.

'Please, Rosa, just listen. You know I am not one for opening up. This is hard for me.'

But he had to try. He could never live with himself if she were to continue believing there was something inherently wrong with her that drove people away.

Lord, what had he done?

His selfish pride and monstrous ego had set off a chain of events he could never have predicted even with the benefit of a crystal ball. Rosa was the last person in the world he would ever want to hurt.

Only when she stilled did Nico resume his thread, uncaring of the rain lashing down on them both. 'You know I grew up without there being any women in my life?'

She nodded jerkily, her hair tickling his face.

'I didn't have my first girlfriend until I was twenty-one. We were together for six months and it is the only proper relationship I have had.'

Somehow her stiff form became even more rigid.

'Galina was the first woman I slept with. Until that point everything I knew about women and relationships came from books. I wanted what the books promised, but I soon learned I am not cut out for relationships. I am incapable of giving a woman what she needs. Galina wanted so much from me and I could not give it to her. I couldn't even spend a night sharing the same bed with her. She was convinced she could change me—I *wanted* her to change me—but it was futile. The more she tried, the more I withdrew. Eventually she'd had enough and walked away, but not before telling me I had something missing.'

Rosa sucked in a breath.

'She was right,' he said. He closed his eyes and inhaled her scent, filling his lungs with her sweetness. 'Galina gave six months of her life to a man who could not reciprocate her love. I wanted to reciprocate but I had never been shown how—and it was too late for me to learn. Non-sexual intimacy leaves me cold. That's why I have always gone with high-maintenance women since. They're so wrapped up in themselves they have nothing to give to anyone else.'

When he'd finished talking he took a deep breath. It was the longest speech he had ever made.

'So why not marry one of them?' she asked.

Slowly she withdrew her arms from around his waist and looked up at him, her eyes scrutinising his face for answers.

'Because I had no wish to tie myself to a woman whose idea of conversation was discussing the latest innovation in self-tanning.' His lips curved a touch. 'I married *you* because you are clever and independent and because you are incredibly beautiful.' The slight smile dropped. 'I also married you because I assumed your aversion to emotional entanglements meant you were the same as me. But you are *not* the same as me. You need someone who can love you and reciprocate the enormous amount of love you have inside you. You need someone who can support you and be a shoulder to lean on.

I can't be that man—I'm not equipped for it. I am too self-ish and controlling and you will be better off without me.'

Even with the rain dripping over her face he could see the tears that continued to fall down her cheeks.

'Come,' he said, hooking an arm around her shoulder. 'We should get inside before we both contract pneumonia.'

'I need to clean up the glass.'

'I'll get a member of the crew to do it.'

'It's no bother.'

'You don't even know where the dustpan is.'

Rosa had no answer to that that. While Nico pressed the buzzer to notify the crew of the shattered glass she slipped away, up the steps to the third deck and into their cabin.

The enormous bed seemed to wink at her.

She didn't even have the energy to flash it the bird. All she wanted was to crash out.

Locking the *en suite* bathroom door behind her, she stripped her sopping clothes off and stood under the shower.

She kept it together, methodically cleaning herself before stepping out and towelling dry. It was not until she stood before the sink to brush her teeth and caught sight of her blurred reflection that her knees gave way and she slumped onto the floor, covering her ears to drown out the scream-ing in her head.

From starting full of such hope and happiness, the day had ended in nothing but darkness.

In its own way, Nico's childhood had been as difficult as her own. Growing up without physical affection had affected him badly, and any chance of him cultivating the semblance of a normal relationship had been snuffed out with one mo-ment of failure.

What kind of twisted world did she live in where she fi-nally found someone she trusted enough to place her heart in his hands only to learn he was unable to care for it? Or was it that he was unwilling to try?

Nico had pulled himself up and created a multi-national empire from nothing but his own blood and sweat. More than anything that proved he had the drive and motivation to succeed when the prize was something he really wanted.

But if there was one thing she knew about her soon-to-be-ex-husband it was that failure would not be tolerated, and being dumped by his first—only—girlfriend would definitely have been classified as failure.

The bloody coward.

'I was getting worried about you,' Nico said when she finally left the bathroom. He was sitting on the edge of the bed, wearing clean, dry shorts. He'd draped a towel over the dressing table chair.

Rosa gazed at him coolly. 'You have nothing to worry about. I just needed some time alone to collect my thoughts.'

For a moment they stared at each other, until he got to his feet. 'You take the bed. I'm going to get some sleep in the saloon.'

It was eerie how similar their thought processes could be. How long had it been since she'd formed her own intention to sleep in the saloon?

Clenching her teeth together, she jerked a nod. 'Take one of the blankets off the bed.'

'No, you'll need it.'

'I'll double the other one up. Please—take it.' Could she *be* any more polite? It certainly beat scratching his eyes out, but it was not, she assumed, half as satisfying.

'If you're sure?'

'I'm sure.' To prove it, she helped him remove the top blanket and folded it together for him, then thrust it with more force than necessary into his arms.

Done, his arms piled with pillows and the blanket, Nico cast her one last look which she was not quick enough to escape from. 'Are you sure you'll be all right on your own?'

'Of course I will.' She forced a smile. 'Goodnight.'

'Goodnight, Rosa.'

Alone, she was all too aware of the ferocious storm raging against the yacht. Yet it was nothing compared to the agonies taking place within her.

Slumping on the bed, she wrapped the remaining blanket around herself, then raised her arm to switch the lights off. Seeing as she had the cabin to herself, she opted to keep the dimmers above the bed on, dulling them to a muted glow.

Without Nico there the mattress felt much too large, as if she could roll over and over and never reach the edge.

Even with all the pillows he had taken there were still half a dozen left for her. She sniffed them in turn. None of them held his scent. Which was a good thing. Why torment herself further? She was no masochist. She hugged one to her chest and tried not to think of how much more comforting it would be if it smelt like her husband.

After two hours spent trying to fall asleep, she was on the verge of screaming or crying. It took everything she had to stop herself doing either.

She had spent the vast majority of her life sleeping alone. She had slept through storms before. Plenty of them.

But no other storm had been so loud. Somehow it was worse being inside and on the top deck. There was hardly anything to muffle the deafening noise.

At least worrying about the storm prevented her from thinking too much about Nico. She really didn't want to think about him, or about the future she had only just accepted could be hers but had been snatched away before she'd had a smidgeon of time to enjoy it.

As the minutes slowly passed the anger that had first

seeded when she had hidden in the bathroom fertilised and began to grow.

Had any of it been real?

They were so good together. As a lover, Nico was incomparable. Or maybe it was her reaction to him that was incomparable?

It had certainly felt real. There had not been an iota of doubt in her mind that the hedonistic rush she had experienced in his arms had been reciprocated. Surely he had not faked his desire for her?

Her experiences with men were limited in the extreme. Stephen had been the first man to get anywhere with her, and it had taken him months of trying for her to agree to a date. After sleeping with him for the first time she had been completely underwhelmed but, having nothing to compare it with, had not been too bothered. She would have been perfectly happy never to see him again but he had been so keen it would have been cruel to end it. Or so she had thought. Maybe it would have been better to have ended it then, before he had time to become more infatuated with her.

She'd never had any illusions, though. Stephen's infatuation had stemmed from her distance. Always he'd tried to chip away at her barriers, but he hadn't been able to smash them down fast enough. Rosa was too accomplished at rebuilding them.

Those barriers had been for her own protection. Being rejected and turned away by her Russian foster mother, a woman she had come to trust and love, had been the last straw. She had sworn *never again*. It had not been conscious. It had been self-protection.

Hindsight was a wonderful thing. Only now could she see how badly she had treated Stephen. She had refused to let him in. And then, after it was all over, she had committed the cardinal sin and—

A bolt of lightning streaked past the yacht, illuminating the cabin in a brief prism of light.

Burying her head under a pillow, she tried to muffle out the storm and her tormented thoughts.

No, she thought. Whatever wrongs she had done to Stephen, surely she did not deserve this burning pain stabbing into her chest, or the nausea just a deep breath away from spilling out? She had never meant to hurt him—especially in the manner she had at their final parting. But she had been so low. So vulnerable. The man she had longed to share her birthday with—her husband—had been too busy to return home. And she had needed human company so badly. With Stephen it had never been real. Not for her.

What she and Nico had shared *had* been real. For two perfect days and nights it had been real. At least for her.

The cabin door opened and she threw the pillow off her head and snapped her head up.

Nico stood at the threshold and gazed at her, his hair sticking up all over the place.

Did he realise his shorts were undone, resting on his hipbones by the slimmest of margins?

For a moment she forgot to breathe.

'I just wanted to check you were okay,' he said, sounding uncomfortable.

'Me? I'm fine.' She didn't know whether she wanted to kiss his face off or throw something at him.

'Liar.' His grin was weak. 'I'll leave you to sleep. Goodnight.'

About to wish him a goodnight in turn, Rosa opened her mouth. 'Was any of it real?'

He cocked his head back. 'Sorry?'

'You and me? What we shared? When me made love? When we explored King Island together? When you treated me like a beautiful princess? Did you mean any of it?'

She watched his magnificent chest rise sharply before he nodded, his eyes a burning fire of intensity. 'It was the best time of my life.'

His chest rose again and he twisted round to leave.

'Don't go.'

'Sorry?'

'Stay with me. Just for tonight.'

Leaning against the doorframe in a pose she found achingly familiar, he lasered her with his eyes, his brow knotted in concentration. 'Do you know what you are asking?'

She nodded.

She knew exactly what she was asking. What they had shared had been the most incredible experience of her life. She had come alive in his arms and it had been glorious. But, more than simply wanting a repeat, she needed to reclaim something. Her pride. This time tomorrow they would be back on Butterfly Island and the forced intimacy between them would be gone. This would be her last chance to let things end on *her* terms. She would no longer allow Nico to dictate everything.

Whether he admitted it to himself or not, he had used her. It had not been intentional, that much she could appreciate, but it did not change the facts. *My definition of that was for us to continue exactly as we were with sex thrown into the mix.* Had he seriously thought she would want a relationship based solely on sex?

All that time and energy he had spent on seducing her she had blithely believed he was attempting to build something special between them.

All that time he had known he would never be able to love her. Not because he was incapable, as he so obviously believed, but because he was too much of a bloody coward even to try.

He had smashed through every one of her defences with

the subtlety of a battering ram but was too scared to put his own defences on the line.

And to her that was unforgiveable.

Well, now it was her turn to use him. But she would not lower herself to using subterfuge. When they went their separate ways she would leave with her head held high.

CHAPTER THIRTEEN

Rosa threw off the sheet and swung her legs off the bed. 'One last time,' she said, padding towards him.

Nico continued to stare at her, immovable, his face unreadable. Except for his eyes. His eyes burned with swirling intensity.

When she reached him, she placed her hands palm-down on his chest, savouring the rapid thrum of his heartbeat.

His chest heaved. His Adam's apple moved as he swallowed.

Looking down, she could see the outline of an erection straining against his shorts. A wave of power rushed through her.

Nico's desire was for *her*.

She lightly traced his smooth skin, the tips of her fingers lacing through the silky black hair, moving on to make circular motions around the dusky nipples which were almost in line with her mouth. Without thinking, she pressed a kiss to one whilst gently pinching the other.

His breathing deepened but he remained still. As she tasted the saltiness of his skin the ache that had lain dormant all day, submerged under a tsunami of anger and grief, roared back to life.

Nico roared back to life too, capturing her cheeks in his

hands and tilting her face upwards. 'You are playing with fire,' he said, his voice a thick groan.

She stared into those magnetic green eyes, which even without the benefit of her glasses were so clearly striking, and slid her hands up and over his shoulders, hooking them around his neck. 'Maybe. But this time I have no intention of getting burned. Now, kiss me.'

Bringing her face close enough to catch the warmth of his breath, he crushed her lips in a kiss that demanded full possession. And full possession was what she gave in return. In the fraction of a second their tongues were duelling, her body flattened against his.

His hands slid away from her face, snaking round to the back of her scalp, where he raked his fingers through her hair before gathering it together.

He broke away and tugged her hair back, angling her chin up. 'Are you sure you want this?'

In answer, she pulled out of his hold and took a step back. She yanked her T-shirt off and threw it on the floor. 'Does this answer your question?'

Witnessing the desire in his eyes sent a powerful bolt of need running through her. She closed the gap between them, deliberately pressing her naked breasts against his bare torso, and squeezed his bottom.

He moved to kiss her again, but she stopped him with a hand to his chest, brushing his nipple with her mouth before covering his entire chest with her lips and tongue, moving lower down to his flat navel, and further still to his low-slung shorts.

When she had first met Nico she had refused to acknowledge the raw masculinity that emanated off him in waves. Somehow she had blanked it out, pretended it didn't exist. Now, the testosterone that seemed to seep out of his pores merged with the feminine hormones *he* had conjured in her and she revelled in his virility, welcomed it as her due.

As his shorts were already unbuttoned, it was a simple matter of tugging the sides to make them drop to his ankles and release his erection, which stood to throbbing attention. Rosa had always considered the male member unsightly, but Nico's was glorious: long and thick and satin-smooth to the touch.

His heavy breathing became ragged when she dropped to her knees and took him inside her mouth, gently cupping his balls as she pleasured him. Or was the pleasure all her own? With every groan that came from his throat, with every dig of his fingers into her scalp, her own need grew.

'God, Rosa,' he said hoarsely, pulling away, although he kept a hand gripped firmly in her hair. 'You're going to make me come.'

'That *is* the point, isn't it?'

He emitted what she assumed to be a laugh before pulling her up onto her feet and stepping out of his shorts. The laughter left his face. 'I want to come in you.'

The moisture that had been bubbling gently at the apex of her thighs heated to an almost unbearable level. Wrapping her arms around his neck, she pressed herself against him, holding on tightly for fear her legs would give way.

Somehow he shuffled them to the bed and laid her down, his mouth reclaiming hers in a fury of passion, arms and legs entwined. Only her lacy knickers provided any barrier to relief. Nico dealt with them the best way: by ripping them off and throwing the scraps to one side. Immediately his hand was *there*, his palm rubbing gently against her bud.

'Spread your legs,' he demanded between kisses when she clamped her thighs together to trap his hand.

She obeyed, spreading her thighs, groaning when he dipped a finger into the hot moistness and increased the friction.

'Go with it,' he urged, then dipped his head to capture a puckered nipple in his mouth, his hand still moving at a steady tempo.

His mouth was everywhere, smothering her breasts, and then his tongue was trailing down to her rounded belly until he was there, replacing his hand with his tongue and burying himself in her heat.

It was too much. Already a burning mass, the pulsating pressure inside her spilt over. Crying out, she arched her back and came in waves of riotous colour.

There was no time for her to glory in the wonder of it. No sooner had the pulsations started to abate than Nico was sheathed—from where, she knew not, and cared even less—and inside her, filling her completely.

She moaned and ran her nails down his back.

He thrust into her, over and over, in a frenzied coupling of pure need. She grabbed his buttocks and drove him deeper, their tongues clashing ferociously as they kissed and nipped and pulled at each other's lips.

He stilled and breathed deeply into her ear. 'I don't want to come yet.' He hooked an arm around her waist and rolled onto his back. Somehow he manoeuvred her with him, without breaking the intimate connection between them, so she was straddling him. His hands rested on her hips. 'I want to watch you come on me.'

His words very nearly did it.

She took a ragged breath and closed her eyes.

Without even realising, she had allowed him to take control again.

Now all the power was back in *her* hands.

She leaned forward to cradle his head in her hands and began to move. She wanted to take her time. Like Nico, she wanted to savour it.

'That's it, my angel, let yourself go.' He captured a breast in his mouth and sucked, sending a bolt of pleasure through to her core.

She ground herself on him, almost flat against him, rubbing their groins together. With his hands at her waist, his tongue making such magic on her nipples and his erection filling her, she forgot herself completely.

How badly she wanted to hold on, to make the most of every thrilling second. But she could not. Nico bucked beneath her, a ring of perspiration breaking out on his brow. He flung his head back and with a cry that seemed to come from his very depths thrust upwards into her, the complete fulfilment and friction sending her over the edge and into the stars.

It took an age before the pulses zipping through every part of her lessened enough for sanity to break free.

She was slumped on him, her face buried in his neck. One of his arms was wrapped tightly around her waist, the other hand making circular motions up and down her back.

She did not want to move. She could happily stay there for ever, locked in his arms in the most intimate way imaginable.

But of course that was impossible.

'Where are you going?' he asked, his voice thick.

'You need to get rid of the condom.' She slid off him and slumped onto her back, taking great pains to keep her voice neutral. 'By the way, where did you get it from?'

'It was on the floor.'

She almost smiled as she recalled him ripping open a large box of them, half the contents spilling everywhere.

He turned onto his side and traced a finger down her stomach. 'I'll be back in a minute.'

Despite herself, she watched his retreating figure stride to the *en suite* bathroom and marvelled anew at the muscular perfection of his broad back, the tight buttocks and the powerful thighs. Oh, but he was perfect. How wonderful it would be to fall asleep wrapped in the security of his arms. It could not happen, though. Not now. It was too late for that.

She expelled a puff of air and wrapped herself in the blanket, closing her eyes when she heard the toilet flush.

When Nico had finished in the bathroom and returned to bed, he found himself confronted by the coldness of Rosa's back. 'Are you all right?'

'Sleepy. G'night.'

Resting on an elbow, he blinked in shock. 'Is that it?'

'It was just sex, Nico. Go to sleep.'

She had to be joking. Except, judging by her low rhythmic breathing, this was no joke.

Whilst disposing of the condom he had mentally braced himself for one more sleep with Rosa wrapped all over him. It had been the strangest feeling ever, sleeping with the warmth of another pressed against him. Instead of withdrawing, as every instinct had told him to do, he had told himself it would be too cruel. The few times he had shifted slightly Rosa had closed the gap in an instant. It was almost as if she had been afraid to lose the physical contact. This from a woman who had always shied away from human affection.

Tonight there was none of that. Her back was firmly placed towards him, cocooned in the blanket. The only thing she hugged was a pillow.

Relief should be coursing through his veins.

So how come the only emotion distinguishable through the rivers raging through him was disappointment?

Ending their marriage was the right decision. Of that he had no doubt. Rosa needed so much more than he could ever give.

As much as it twisted his guts and made his skin feel as if a nest of wasps were freely stinging him, he prayed with every fibre of his being that she would find it.

* * *

Rosa trained the powerful binoculars on Butterfly Island. Without them it was but a speck in the distance. With them she could see the mountainous backdrop and its verdant greenery darkening as the sun made its descent. It wouldn't be long now.

For once she had risen before Nico. She had deliberately left him sleeping. She'd had no wish for a post-mortem on her behaviour in the early hours of the morning. She still didn't know where that wantonness had come from, but she did not regret it.

Nico had hurt her. Really hurt her. It was as if he had reached a hand into her heart and ripped it out without anaesthetic. Making love on *her* terms had done little to mitigate the hurt, but it had allowed her to regain some control. Turning her back on him had felt like a fitting finale.

The more she played events in her head—over and over, as if on a loop—the higher her temperature rose. Whilst she felt desperately sorry for the pain he had gone through, and the experiences that had shaped him into the man he was today, she struggled to forgive him.

Her initial instincts had proven correct. Nico had played with her as if she were an unwanted toy another child had tried to steal. Before she had told him about Stephen and asked for a divorce his interest in her sexually had been zero. He'd liked their marriage because it suited *him*. He'd decided to have sex with her because it suited *him*.

Not once had he asked himself if it suited her too.

No, Mr Arrogant had not bothered to look beyond the surface. He had assumed she would be happy to continue in a loveless, emotionless marriage as long as he took care of her physical needs. As soon as he'd discovered she was more complicated than he had credited, he'd done a U-turn so swift her neck had almost cricked again.

He wasn't even prepared to try forging a proper relationship, and he had twisted this cowardice to make it sound s if he was doing her a favour.

Last night she had made love to him because it had suited *her.* For once she had put her own needs first. And now her hurt was gone. Other than what she considered to be justifiable anger she felt nothing. All that resided inside her was a black void.

Her anger abated slightly into concern a short while later, when Nico came into the saloon from their cabin, where he had been changing before they docked, his phone clutched in his hand. One look at his ashen face was enough for her to know something was wrong.

'What's the matter?' she asked, half rising from the table she was sitting at.

He slumped into the chair opposite her and dragged a hand down his face. 'My father's had a stroke. They don't think he's going to make it.'

Thank God for Rosa.

As Nico was driven from Moscow airport to the private hospital holding his father, the image of his wife's calm efficiency soothed him.

He had never before understood the saying *A burden shared is a burden halved.* Now he did. Rosa had immediately comprehended the urgency of the situation and, breaking him out of his stupor, had set up a plan of action. He'd had no hesitation in granting her Power of Attorney. The contracts with Robert King would go ahead with Rosa's signature on the documents.

Knowing his business could not be in better hands had freed him to concentrate on the minutiae of his travel arrangements. The doctor had told him in no uncertain terms

they were talking *days*. At the most. It had been imperative
to become airborne as soon as possible.

Now, as the car pulled up alongside the hospital entrance,
he knew his debt to Rosa could never be repaid. His father
was hanging on. Because of Rosa Nico would be given the
opportunity to say goodbye to the man who had given him
life and raised him.

An austere nurse was waiting for him at the main door. Her
calm efficiency reminded him of Rosa. He followed her down
wide corridors to a wing that was as silent as it was stark. He
had spent the day-long journey mentally preparing himself
for what he was about to see, but when the nurse opened the
door to his father's private room he realised all the time in
the world could not have prepared him.

His father, a person he always envisaged in his mind's eye
as a giant of a man, had shrivelled. His skin—what could be
seen of it behind all the tubes and the oxygen mask connected
to him—had become translucent and had a powdery hue to
it. When he pressed his fingers gently to the cool forehead
he half expected a residue to adhere to the tips.

Mikhail Baranski opened his eyes.

Nico had to act quickly to smother his shock. All his father's vibrancy had gone. It looked as if someone had placed
Clingfilm over his eyeballs.

Through the mask Nico could see his father trying to talk.
As far as he was aware Mikhail had not uttered a word since
the stroke occurred.

'I am going to take the mask off,' he said to the nurse who
was hovering behind him.

'That is not advisable.'

He quelled her with a look. 'I wasn't asking permission.'

If she'd wanted to argue about it, whatever she saw in
Nico's eyes warned her of the futility. Instead she turned on

her heel and left the room—no doubt to find a doctor and report him.

Alone with his father, Nico pulled a chair as close as he could to the bed without knocking any of the equipment and took a seat. He lifted the mask, taking care not to remove it completely.

'Nicolai?' Only the right-hand side of Mikhail's mouth worked, and his words were a laborious slur.

'I'm here, Papa,' he said, clasping his fingers around Mikhail's withered hand.

The shrunken chest heaved. 'Your wife? Here?'

'Rosa?' Nico had to fight the instinct to squeeze his fingers at the mention of her. His father felt so fragile he feared he would snap the bones in his hand. 'No, she's not here.'

The filmy eyes blinked. Was that reproach he detected in them?

And then it came to him. The last time he had seen his father a few short months ago he had promised he would bring Rosa on his next visit. In one of his more sober moments Mikhail had confessed a longing to meet his daughter-in-law. Nico had thought it wise not to confide that his marriage was one of convenience. He'd had a gut feeling his father would not approve.

Mikhail took another deep breath. 'Picture?'

'You want to see a picture of Rosa?'

A blink.

'Let me check my wallet.' He knew the gesture was pointless. Why would he carry a picture of Rosa with him? But to say that would be cruel.

After replacing the oxygen mask securely, he dug into his back pocket and pulled out his wallet. He opened it and pretended to rummage through it, stopping short when his fingers brushed the creased edge of a photo he had not looked at properly for a decade.

With hands that were not quite steady he pulled it out and stared at the faded picture of his mother. The colour quality had dulled dramatically over the years, but nothing could diminish the vibrancy of her ebony hair or the sweetness of her smile.

'I'm sorry, Papa,' he said quietly. 'I don't seem to have a picture of Rosa on me.'

Mikhail's eyes fixed on the small photo in Nico's hands.

'It's a picture of Mama,' he explained, turning it over and bringing it close to his father's eyes.

For an age nothing was said. He was about to place it back in his wallet when a tear leaked down Mikhail's sunken cheek.

'Papa?'

The filmy eyes were fixed back on him, beseeching him.

Understanding his father was trying to talk, Nico removed the mask again.

'Katerina.' His mother's name came out like a long, rattly sigh.

His chest tight, unsure if he was doing the right thing, Nico held the picture inches from his father's face.

A light came into his father's eyes, and a look of contentment stole across the distorted face. Mikhail drew in another long whistling breath. 'My Katerina.'

Such was his father's stillness as he stared at the thirty-five-year-old picture that for the time it took his heart to leap into his mouth and begin to choke him Nico feared he had slipped away.

Only when the filmy eyes blinked and refocused on him did Nico start to breathe again. In his heart he knew it wouldn't be long. The time elapsing between each rattling, whistling breath was increasing. His father could not hold on much more.

Placing his mother's picture on the pillow, he leaned over

and, for the very first time, pressed his lips to his father's forehead. His senses were consumed with a scent that was both familiar and yet also wholly unknown—a scent that clutched at him and twisted his guts. 'I love you, Papa.'

But Mikhail was spent. As he struggled to form words with lips that no longer worked Nico placed a finger to them.

'It's all right. I know you love me. You've always loved me.'

And as he looked into the diminishing light of his father's eyes—eyes that contained such love and, strangely, such peace—he knew it to be true. He could feel it in every atom of his being.

Rosa's words came back to him. *'It took guts for him to keep you. He must love you very much.'*

His beautiful Rosa. A woman who had known such darkness, yet had thrown off the shackles of fear and reached for the light. A woman who had reached into his black heart and coloured it. The woman whose face was the very one he would want to see when the time came for *him* to leave this earth.

Mikhail's eyes were no longer seeing. Even so, Nico held his mother's picture before him and stroked the cooling forehead, the tears pouring down his cheeks falling like rain, soaking them both.

CHAPTER FOURTEEN

ROSA READ THE message one more time.

I'll be back in London early tomorrow evening. There are things we need to discuss. Appreciate you meeting me at the house. Regards, Nico.

'Tomorrow evening' had now arrived, and as she punched in the security code at the gate with clammy fingers she felt all *bitty*—as if the working parts of her body had fragmented and none of the connecting parts knew how to work together any more.

This would be the first time she had seen him since Butterfly Island. He had been in Moscow for the past ten days, dealing with his father's funeral and sorting out the legalities.

In all the conversations they'd had since he'd left, only one had driven into personal territory. Nico had called her shortly after his father had passed away. He had wanted to thank her. His voice had been so bereft that she had felt any residue of anger vanish on the spot. Well, most of it had. It had been hard to hold on to it after witnessing the sheer devastation in his eyes when he had told her of his father's stroke.

But she needed that tiny residue. Without it a black pit of despair beckoned, and she couldn't afford to fall into it.

Even so, she had been unable to hold back the tears. When

the call had ended she had sunk onto the floor and cried for them—for the future they would never have—and then she had cried for Nico and his father. The urge to get the soonest flight to Moscow so she could be there for him had at times overwhelmed her. The day of Mikhail Baranski's funeral had been especially hard to endure. Thinking of Nico grieving alone had cut her like ribbons. *She should have been with him.*

But he'd relied on her to see the deal with Robert King through, and she had been determined to see it through properly. In any case, he wouldn't have wanted her there—not his soon-to-be-ex-wife.

In the end, the contracts had been signed without any fuss. Robert had been as determined to see as smooth a progression as she was. Six days later she had returned to the UK to step into Nico's shoes at his London office. Since then all their conversations had been entirely work-related.

Intuition told her this meeting was *not* work-related. This was personal. This could only be about their divorce.

She drove through the gate and parked on the gravel at the front of the house.

The front door swung open before she could climb the steps.

'Hello, Rosa.'

Her heart tripped. She paused and gazed at him. 'Hello, Nico.'

As all her recent memories were of him wearing shorts and nothing else, it was startling to see him decked out in an impeccably ironed white shirt and grey trousers. They provided a stark contrast with the rumpled look of his face. With large bags under his bloodshot eyes, he looked as if he hadn't slept in months. His hair was as messy as ever, which she found strangely comforting.

'Why haven't you parked in the garage?'

'It seemed a bit pointless, seeing as I shan't be staying

long.' At least she *hoped* she wouldn't be staying too long. At that moment she was doing an admirable imitation of nonchalance, but it was hurting every sinew in her body to keep it up.

Work, as always, had been her salvation. Throwing herself into the contracts and then ensuring Nico's empire ran smoothly in his unexpected absence had enabled her to push aside all the pain. And if she'd lived on a diet of strong coffee, unable to stomach food in a belly that ached, then so be it. Anything had to better than having time to think.

Now, standing before him, she was overwhelmed with how badly she had missed him.

He inclined his head and stood aside to admit her.

'Where's Gloria?' she asked, automatically kicking her shoes off as she stepped into the reception room. For a split-second she searched for her slippers, before remembering they were at the hotel she would call home for the next few weeks, until she could move back into her old flat.

She hadn't been able to face returning to the empty house. Gloria had kindly brought all her possessions to the hotel for her. If she had an opinion on Rosa moving out, she had kept it to herself.

'I sent her home,' Nico said.

She followed him into the kitchen, blinking in disbelief. She hadn't expected them to be alone.

'It's all right,' Nico said, correctly reading her thoughts. 'I wanted some privacy for our talk. Coffee? Or something stronger?'

'Seeing as I'm driving, I'll have coffee, thank you. Instant will be fine.' She didn't want to hang around while he faffed with the percolator. She wanted to get this conversation over with and return to the privacy of her hotel room and lick her wounds.

While he made their drinks she could not help but gaze at him. He turned his head and caught her staring.

Something intangible yet very real passed between them—
something that pulled and tugged inside her. He had lost
weight. She was certain of it.

'How are you? I mean really?' she asked softly.

His lips curved into a rueful smile. 'Better now you're
here.'

Before she could react to that answer, he'd turned back and
poured the boiling water into cups, giving both a vigorous stir.

He picked them up and walked past her. 'Let's go and sit
in the living room.'

Rosa took her usual seat on the far sofa and waited for Nico
to take *his* usual seat opposite, with the coffee table dividing
them. Instead, after setting their drinks down, he took the
armchair closest to her.

'How did the funeral go?' It was something she had wanted
to ask for days, but as he had led all the conversations between
them since and kept them on a strict work footing, the moment had never felt right. She half expected him to dismiss
the question now and dive straight into their divorce talks.

'It was very nice,' he said, before adding heavily, 'If a funeral can ever be described as *nice*. A lot of people came.'
His eyes lightened at the reminiscence. 'The church was full
of drunks. At one point I thought they would throw empty
bottles instead of dirt onto the coffin.'

She snickered before she could stop herself, relieved he
could still find some sunshine at such an awful time. 'I really am sorry.'

'I know you are. But he is happy now. He's where he's
wanted to be for over three decades. With my mother.' He
sighed heavily and reached for his coffee. 'When I was sorting through his stuff I discovered boxes he had kept that I
did not know existed. They were full of love letters and me-
mentoes, all between him and my mother.'

Resting his elbows on his knees, he took a sip of the scalding coffee.

'I also found the diary he kept for the first few years after she died. It made illuminating reading. All my life I assumed he drank out of boredom. I knew he was an alcoholic, but I always thought the root cause of it...' He shook his head. 'He never got over her death. He drank to numb the pain. Raising me was the only thing that got him out of bed in the morning.'

Rosa sat ramrod-straight, hardly daring to breathe, afraid to utter a word. Despite their impending divorce, Nico was sharing confidences out of choice. A huge part of her yearned to wrap her arms around him, hold him close and soothe all his pain away.

He fixed his beautiful, tired green eyes on her and smiled. 'Don't be sad for him, or for me. He is with her now, and there is no other place he would rather be. He left this world happy his only son had settled. His only regret—*my* only regret— was that he never got to meet you.'

He must have seen the shock she was not quick enough to hide. 'I told him all about you—about your intelligence and your sense of fair play and your refusal to judge people.' His lips quirked. 'Unless they look like supermodels.' His features straightened, his eyes penetrating. 'I never cared to think of the reasons why you shied away from women like that. I was so self-absorbed at the beginning of our marriage it never occurred to me there was an underlying reason for your insecurity.'

'Other than being an unremarkable frump?' she couldn't resist retorting, thrown completely off-balance at this turn in the conversation.

Her equilibrium was knocked further off-kilter when he reached over and pressed a warm hand to her neck. 'If it takes the rest of my life I swear one day you will look in the mirror and see the beauty *my* eyes see when they look at you.'

'You don't have to try and sweet-talk me,' she said, edging away from him. 'Not any more.'

'I'm not trying to sweet-talk you.'

'Then what *are* you doing?'

He closed his eyes, then placed his cup on the table and moved to the sofa next to her, his thigh brushing against hers. When he spoke, his voice was low. 'I need to ask you something and I want you to promise to tell me the truth.' He grabbed her hand and placed it on his lap. 'Promise me the truth, Rosa.'

It was the urgency in his voice that made her nod her agreement. She had not the faintest idea what could be so important. 'I promise.'

'Why did you really go out with Stephen on your birthday? And why did it end so badly?'

He might as well have stuck a pin in her. Slumping back, she closed her eyes.

'Look at me,' he commanded. 'I need to know. It matters a great deal to me.'

'Why?' she whispered, keeping her eyes shut.

'Because ever since you told me you slept with your ex it has felt as if my stomach has had acid thrown into it.'

She tried frantically to swallow away the brick that had lodged in her throat. Of all the things he could ask her, why this? And why now? And what the heck did he mean about acid?

'You promised.'

His deep voice rumbled in her ear.

'Please, Rosa. I need to know.'

'I went out with Stephen because I was hurt that you stood me up. Actually, scratch that. I was *devastated* that you stood me up.' There. She had dredged the words out.

She waited for him to respond, but after a few too many seconds of silence she opened her eyes. Nico, his face inches from her own, was staring at her with an intensity she had never seen before.

He slowly inclined his head. 'Go on.'

'It wasn't just about you,' she admitted with a sigh. 'Although that was a big factor in it. I'd been feeling low—I'd made contact with my brother...'

'You did what?'

'I contacted my brother.'

'You never told me.'

She shrugged helplessly. 'You weren't there to tell. And it was personal—not part of our deal, remember?'

It was Nico's turn to close his eyes. 'I remember.'

'I'd convinced myself that now he was an adult he might want to get to know his big sister. So I wrote to him asking to meet up.'

'What happened?'

'He texted me back. He said he was very busy, but if he ever found the time he would get in touch.' She expelled air through her nose and shook her head. 'He blew me out. He didn't want to know me any more than our mother did when she was alive.'

It was only when Rosa yelped that Nico realised he was squeezing her hand hard enough to cause her pain. 'I'm sorry,' he muttered, removing it and placing it very carefully on her thigh.

Every time he heard about the callous treatment meted out to her by her so-called family he wanted to punch something to ease the rage that screamed through his blood.

He knew how much it must have cost her to write to her brother in the first place and what a low place she must have been in even to go down that route. He could only imagine the torment she'd suffered when her brother rejected her too.

What was *wrong* with these people? How could they treat their own flesh and blood with such cruel indifference?

Very soon he would tell her something that should ease the suffering caused by those bastards, tell her that his Australian investigator had found her great-aunt Myra and that Myra wanted to meet her. But first, selfish as he knew he was being, he needed to hear the rest of it.

'How soon before your birthday did all this happen?' He traced his fingers lightly over her hand, his chest constricting when he realised she had removed her wedding ring.

Its absence felt like a punch in the gut.

'A week or so.'

A week. A whole week for it to fester before he had called on the day of her birthday and told her he wouldn't be able to make it home. His cowardice at a time when she'd needed him had driven her into the arms of another.

No wonder she had removed her ring. He was only surprised she hadn't removed it sooner. It would have been no more than he deserved.

'I'm sorry. I should have been there.'

'Why? How could you have known? It wasn't—'

'I know: it wasn't part of our pact,' he finished for her, before confessing, 'I could have made it back if I had wanted to. I already knew a couple of days before your birthday that I wouldn't be investing in the Moroccan site.'

'Oh.'

The feeling of her shriveling next to him splintered through him like shattered glass. Any guilt he had felt was magnified by a hundred. 'I kept dreaming of you.'

'Oh?'

Nico laughed mirthlessly. He had known this evening would be difficult. He had also known the only way they could forge a future together—a proper future—was to lay all their cards on the table. Reading through the letters exchanged between his parents, learning of the strength of their devotion to each other and seeing the sheer honesty in the emotions on the page had been a revelation. Nothing had been held back between them.

Now he and Rosa had to find that level of emotional honesty. As Rosa knew to her cost, the spoken word could cause irreparable damage. But, as he had come to realise over recent times, the unspoken word could cause just as much harm.

He drained his coffee and turned to face her. Unable to resist, he palmed her cheek, taking comfort from its softness. 'When you told me you'd slept with Stephen I felt sucker-punched.'

Her warm caramel eyes widened a fraction.

'Forget all the excuses I've made to you and myself. The truth is I've used Galina as an excuse to avoid proper relationships because I tasted failure and I did not like it. Until then I had never failed at anything I set my mind to. I assumed my coldness was a result of my childhood, and I accepted that and used it as weapon to prevent myself from tasting failure again. Looking back, I can see it never occurred to me my ambivalence towards Galina was because I was not in love with her.'

Rosa's forehead wrinkled in that adorable manner it always did when she tried to comprehend something.

'I spent months denying I felt any attraction for you. Your refusal to work for me permanently was, I admit, a blow to my ego, but with hindsight I can see it was more than that. I knew I had no proprietary rights over you, but I have never felt such anger and such pain as I did in those minutes when I thought you were leaving me for Stephen.'

'But—'

'Please, let me finish,' he said, brushing her lips with his thumb. 'We had agreed to what should be every red-blooded man's dream—an open marriage. It didn't even occur to me until you told me you wanted to leave that I'd never made use of that freedom.'

If her eyes widened any further he feared they might pop out.

'What? Never?'

He shook his head solemnly. 'Never. There were opportunities, but I never felt the slightest urge to act on them. Since we married you have been the only woman in my head. There is no room for anyone else. I can fight it all I want—and, believe me, I have been fighting it hard—but it doesn't change the facts. Somewhere over the past year you have crept under my skin and into my heart.'

It twisted that heart to watch her blink rapidly, trying her best to hold back the tears brimming in her eyes.

'Why are you telling me all this?' she asked, her chin wobbling.

'Because I love you. And I want you to come home. Not because of work, not because I want to make love to you every hour of the day—which I do—but because living without you is torture.' As the words rolled off his tongue a huge weight shifted in its vice-like hold on his chest.

A solitary tear rolled down her cheek. She wiped it away in a furious motion. 'You are a complete and utter bastard.'

'Yes.' He could not deny it.

'And a coward.'

'Yes.'

'You really hurt me.'

'I know.' Imagining what he had put her through cut him like ribbons. 'I swear I will spend the rest of my life making it up to you. If you will let me.'

He swallowed, waiting for her to speak.

He had known laying his heart on the line was a risk. He had known it could end in failure. But not trying was no longer an option. He needed Rosa. Without her by his side it had become impossible to function properly.

Time stretched beyond all measure. The only sound was their quickening breaths.

'I called him by your name,' she blurted out, her neck suffused with colour.

He stilled. 'Sorry?'

'It was horrible. I should never have gone back to his flat. I should never have...' Her voice tailed off and she swallowed. When she spoke again her voice was a whisper. 'We never finished what we started. I only endured what we *did* do by closing my eyes and pretending he was you. And then I called him by your name. And he got understandably angry and threw me out.'

Shock paralysed him. For long moments his brain struggled to understand what she had said. 'He threw you out? On the street? In London? In the middle of the night?'

She nodded and wiped away another tear with a scowl. 'I can't blame him. He assumed I was going back to him. When he realised I was in love with you...'

His pulse accelerated. 'You *love* me?'

'Of course I love you,' she whispered, her face white and pinched. 'I think I've been in love with you since we married.'

Now it was his brain struggling to comprehend. 'So why ask for a divorce?'

'Because I knew staying with you would destroy me. I knew I was nothing but a convenience. Going with Stephen that night, as horrible as it was, made me realise how much I felt for you. Every time you went abroad the loneliness became unbearable.' She shook her head wistfully. 'You had become so...ambivalent towards me. Thinking you felt nothing for me, imagining all the women you were sharing your bed with and thinking you would never look at me with the need I felt for you...' Her eyes closed. 'I couldn't bear it.'

He could hold on no more. Wrapping an arm around her, he pulled her to him and held her tightly, inhaling that sweet scent he had so missed. 'I love you, Rosa Baranski. You have no idea how much. You are everything to me.'

She expelled a sigh and tilted her face to look at him. 'I love you too. More than anything.'

'I'm scared,' he finally admitted, his chest heaving with the words.

'Of what?'

'Hurting you.

'You've already done that and I'm still standing. And, Nico, you can't put all the blame on your own shoulders. We're as bad as each other at keeping things internalised.'

'Not any more,' he vowed, clutching her hand and pressing it against his chest.

He had always needed his physical and mental space. And yet after spending three nights sharing a bed with Rosa sleeping alone had felt...well, *wrong* was the only way he could describe the strangeness of it all. And who else had he ever felt compelled to confide in? Who else's opinion did he value? No one. Just Rosa. Just his wife.

But what if he slipped back into his old, cold ways? He could not stomach the thought of causing her further pain. She had suffered enough in her life. They both had.

He'd closed his eyes when she palmed his cheek in turn. 'Nico, look at me,' she commanded in a tone she must have picked up from him.

When he opened them, he found her eyes full of such softness and love he feared his chest would burst from the pressure inside it.

'I am not expecting miracles and neither should you,' she said gently. 'You are who you are, and I wouldn't change anything about you—not even your bastard tendencies. Just as I am who *I* am, with all my insecurities. As long as we love each other, and are honest and committed to *us*, we can work anything out.'

His chest expanded at the faith and love reflecting from her eyes.

'It feels as if I have spent my entire life alone,' he said, keeping her hand tight against his chest, certain she could feel the hammering of his heart. 'But I never felt lonely. It wasn't until you left that I realised how empty and cold my life really was and how much I needed you. Without you, nothing is the same. Everything is wrong. You, *daragaya*, are everything to me.'

Her eyes didn't waver. 'And *you* are everything to me. You make me whole.'

He gripped her hand even tighter, his finger grazing the spot where her wedding ring should be. 'Marry me.'

Her brows furrowed into a question.

'Marry me—let's renew our wedding vows and do it properly this time. And this time the rings we exchange will mean everything they should have done when we first did it.'

Rosa's smile could have illuminated an entire city. 'I can't think of anything I want more. Yes. A hundred times yes.'

Hands snaking around each other's necks, they pulled together into a kiss full of such love and hope the last residue of self-doubt was dislodged and their hearts became complete.

* * * * *

Mills & Boon® Hardback

August 2013

ROMANCE

The Billionaire's Trophy	Lynne Graham
Prince of Secrets	Lucy Monroe
A Royal Without Rules	Caitlin Crews
A Deal with Di Capua	Cathy Williams
Imprisoned by a Vow	Annie West
Duty At What Cost?	Michelle Conder
The Rings that Bind	Michelle Smart
An Inheritance of Shame	Kate Hewitt
Faking It to Making It	Ally Blake
Girl Least Likely to Marry	Amy Andrews
The Cowboy She Couldn't Forget	Patricia Thayer
A Marriage Made in Italy	Rebecca Winters
Miracle in Bellaroo Creek	Barbara Hannay
The Courage To Say Yes	Barbara Wallace
All Bets Are On	Charlotte Phillips
Last-Minute Bridesmaid	Nina Harrington
Daring to Date Dr Celebrity	Emily Forbes
Resisting the New Doc In Town	Lucy Clark

MEDICAL

Miracle on Kaimotu Island	Marion Lennox
Always the Hero	Alison Roberts
The Maverick Doctor and Miss Prim	Scarlet Wilson
About That Night...	Scarlet Wilson

0713 GEN STD HB

Mills & Boon® Large Print
August 2013

ROMANCE

Master of her Virtue	Miranda Lee
The Cost of her Innocence	Jacqueline Baird
A Taste of the Forbidden	Carole Mortimer
Count Valieri's Prisoner	Sara Craven
The Merciless Travis Wilde	Sandra Marton
A Game with One Winner	Lynn Raye Harris
Heir to a Desert Legacy	Maisey Yates
Sparks Fly with the Billionaire	Marion Lennox
A Daddy for Her Sons	Raye Morgan
Along Came Twins...	Rebecca Winters
An Accidental Family	Ami Weaver

HISTORICAL

The Dissolute Duke	Sophia James
His Unusual Governess	Anne Herries
An Ideal Husband?	Michelle Styles
At the Highlander's Mercy	Terri Brisbin
The Rake to Redeem Her	Julia Justiss

MEDICAL

The Brooding Doc's Redemption	Kate Hardy
An Inescapable Temptation	Scarlet Wilson
Revealing The Real Dr Robinson	Dianne Drake
The Rebel and Miss Jones	Annie Claydon
The Son that Changed his Life	Jennifer Taylor
Swallowbrook's Wedding of the Year	Abigail Gordon

3 GEN STD LP

Mills & Boon® Hardback
September 2013

ROMANCE

Challenging Dante	Lynne Graham
Captivated by Her Innocence	Kim Lawrence
Lost to the Desert Warrior	Sarah Morgan
His Unexpected Legacy	Chantelle Shaw
Never Say No to a Caffarelli	Melanie Milburne
His Ring Is Not Enough	Maisey Yates
A Reputation to Uphold	Victoria Parker
A Whisper of Disgrace	Sharon Kendrick
If You Can't Stand the Heat...	Joss Wood
Maid of Dishonour	Heidi Rice
Bound by a Baby	Kate Hardy
In the Line of Duty	Ami Weaver
Patchwork Family in the Outback	Soraya Lane
Stranded with the Tycoon	Sophie Pembroke
The Rebound Guy	Fiona Harper
Greek for Beginners	Jackie Braun
A Child to Heal Their Hearts	Dianne Drake
Sheltered by Her Top-Notch Boss	Joanna Neil

MEDICAL

The Wife He Never Forgot	Anne Fraser
The Lone Wolf's Craving	Tina Beckett
Re-awakening His Shy Nurse	Annie Claydon
Safe in His Hands	Amy Ruttan